Where She Belongs

Suite 300 - 990 Fort St
Victoria, BC, V8V 3K2
Canada

www.friesenpress.com

First Edition — 2019

ISBN
978-1-5255-5577-0 (Hardcover)
978-1-5255-5578-7 (Paperback)
978-1-5255-5579-4 (eBook)

1. FICTION, ROMANCE, CONTEMPORARY

Distributed to the trade by The Ingram Book Company

Where She Belongs

KAITLIN COOKE

Chapter One

AMELIA

Music blasting, the windows down, and hair blowing in the wind. The sun beats down on the open road. Sounds perfect, doesn't it?

I wasn't sure where I was headed when I jumped in my car yesterday afternoon, but twenty-six hours and three gas stops later, I crossed over the state line into Texas. It's a long drive from New York. My funeral dress is wrinkled, and I'm pretty sure I smell like ass. All I've eaten since I left the cemetery was a bag of Cheetos I picked up at the gas station.

It's been ten years since I was last in Sierra Blanca, Texas, but even in the setting sun everything looks the same. It's a very small town with only a half-dozen stores all privately owned by local families. There isn't even a chain grocery store. You'd have to drive the hour to El Paso if you wanted any metropolitan experience.

Despite never having personally driven in the town, my memory leads me past the residential district and out to the rural farmlands without error. Miles of desert separate the farms as I draw closer to the mountains. I keep my eyes trained on the road as I pass the sign for the ranch my family used to own. I turn off at the next dirt road and bump along until I reach the driveway of a large ranch-style home. The sun has set, so lights shine out the windows of both the house and the guesthouse.

The thought doesn't even cross my mind that he won't recognize me as I trudge across the rutted dirt lot. My heels keep getting stuck in the mud, so I pull them off and continue on barefoot. I knock on the door to the guesthouse without hesitation. I know he's in there.

I hear the familiar sound of cowboy boots on hardwood as he approaches. The door swings open, and there he stands, bare-chested and glorious. His blonde hair bleached from the sun is shorter than I'm used to, and his scrawny body has morphed into a chiselled wall of muscle with broad shoulders and washboard abs. His crystal-blue eyes, however, are exactly the same. I watch as his blank expression flickers to something more like disbelief.

"Amelia?" The tattoos on his arms ripple with the flex of his muscles as he runs his hand through his messy hair.

"Dawson," I answer. A wave of tears erupts and I'm a snivelling mess for the first time since I found my father dead five days ago.

"I am so sorry." Dawson takes a step forward and envelops me in a hug. My tears plaster my face to his chest, but I don't care. He scoops me up and carries me as a sobbing bundle into the guesthouse, kicking the door closed with his foot.

"I only heard yesterday, otherwise I would have came out for the funeral," Dawson says as he effortlessly climbs the stairs and enters the bedroom. He lays me down on the bed and then takes a step back, crossing his arms over his chest.

"Amelia, does anybody know you're here?" he asks. I pull my knees up to my chest and wrap my arms around them. I shake my head.

"People are probably worried about you," he starts, but the words drift off as he thinks better of it. "What are you doing here?"

"I didn't have anywhere else to go," I reply, my voice muffled by my knees.

"What about school? You are still in school, aren't you?"

"I graduated from the School of American Ballet two years ago. I'm with New York City Ballet now," I correct him.

"Right, well, don't you need to be there?"

"It was a mistake to come here—I don't know why I thought you'd care." I stand up and straighten my dress before making for the door.

"Amelia, stop. You know that's not what I meant." Dawson's hand wraps around my arm.

"Everyone calls me Ame." I don't turn to face him; my hand lingers over the doorknob. According to my classmates 'Amelia' is too old fashioned. They began shortening it to Amy with an 'e' and it stuck. I'm not even sure the people I've met since know that it's short for something.

"Well, I call you Amelia, and I'm sorry, but I haven't laid eyes on you in ten years. You ran away and completely cut me off, so forgive me if I'm a little thrown by your sudden appearance."

"I didn't run away." I'm still staring down the door; his hand is still on my arm.

"It sure seems like you did. Your mother died, and next thing I know you're packing up to move across the country and nobody hears from you again." Dawson gently pulls on my arm, so I spin to face him.

"I left so that I could pursue a career in ballet. It was my father's idea."

"Are you sure it was his idea? You could have gone to a fancy school right here in Texas. Why so far away?"

"Maybe Dad and I needed space. I don't know! It was so long ago now, but it probably had something to do with the fact that my father only moved here to be with my mother. When she was killed, he had no reason to stay, so why be surrounded by constant reminders if he didn't have to be? Maybe *I* was his excuse to leave! We will never know, because now he's dead too. Everyone's fucking dead!"

"I'm so sorry, Amelia." He pulls me into him again but I resist, pounding his chest with my fists, but my tiny frame is nothing compared to the strength of his arms locked around me.

"I don't know what I'm doing, or why. My mind is spinning a hundred miles an hour and I can't get it to stop." I cry into his shoulder as my strength ebbs and my hands fall to my sides.

"Look at me." Dawson lifts my chin with his finger so that my eyes meet his. He slowly lowers his lips to mine, his eyes asking permission. I answer by stretching up onto my toes, crushing my mouth to his. One of his hands finds the curve of my back while the other weaves his fingers through my hair.

"Dawson," I whimper as he nibbles on my lip. His mouth leaves mine so that he can plant a trail of kisses along my jaw over to my ear, where he sucks on the lobe. I slip my fingers through the belt loops of his jeans so I can pull his hips closer. The hand on my back slides down to my ass and gives me a boost so I can wrap my legs around his waist. Trudging over to the bed, he lays me down on my back and lowers himself on top of me.

"Has your mind slowed down at all?" Dawson pulls away from me slightly so that he can gaze down at me.

"No, but in a good way," I respond, breathless.

"Good." He knots his hands back into my hair and his tongue dances with mine. My fingers find his belt, and I'm in the process of undoing it when the door opens downstairs.

"Dawson?" a female voice calls up over the stairs.

"Shit," he curses and rolls off of me.

"Do you have a girlfriend?" I ask, pulling away from him to sit at the top of the bed.

"No, just a friend," he mutters, standing up and fixing his belt.

"Whose car is that?" The voice is climbing the stairs.

"Kind of busy at the moment, Harper." Dawson opens the door just as she's about to turn the knob. She steps back, surprised.

"Oh, well, I guess that answers my question." The girl blushes and averts her eyes.

"Sorry, Harper. Amelia showed up and I totally forgot," Dawson apologizes.

"Of course you did. I'll just leave you two to it then." Without looking at me, Harper turns and hurries back down the stairs.

"Fuck." Dawson grabs a shirt off his dresser and hurries after her.

I listen as the door slams downstairs, opens, and then slams again as Dawson tries to catch up with Harper. I sit in the silence not totally understanding what has just happened. She seemed awful upset for someone who wasn't his girlfriend. Pulling my phone from my purse, I scan all the missed texts and calls I still haven't answered from as far back as yesterday morning. Turning it off, I throw it on his bedside table, get up, and rummage around until I find the drawer containing Dawson's older shirts. Stepping out of my dress, I slip on the massive T-shirt and crawl under the covers. I turn off the light and snuggle into the bed, which is saturated with his smell. It doesn't take long for me to fall asleep.

DAWSON

Harper's truck skids out of the driveway before I have a chance to start my own. By the time I reach the road, I can't even see her taillights anymore. Figuring she needs space anyway, I return my truck to the spot next to Amelia's fancy car.

Harper had recently gotten a horse that was being kept at a boarding stable across town. I was supposed to show her tonight how to properly remove horseshoes, clean up the hooves, and then reshoe. With Amelia's sudden arrival, I had totally forgotten about our plans. Don't get me wrong: Harper is a really sweet girl. I also know she's had a crush on me for years, which I haven't exactly deterred. But I will always drop anyone and everything for Amelia.

In saying that, I know I shouldn't be messing with Amelia, especially after the death of her father. I wasn't expecting her to come to me for comfort. It's been ten years since I last saw her, aside from being an occasional Facebook creep. So instead of going back into the house, I head to the barn to take my horse out for a ride.

A couple hours later, I figure Amelia's asleep so I creep into my house. Sure enough, she's curled up in the bed wearing one of my shirts. The pillow is soaked with her tears, and I feel awful for leaving her here alone, but at the same time I need to keep my distance. Once the grief has passed she'll return to New York and break my heart all over again.

Shoving some stuff into a bag, I head out to the barn; I figure I'll sleep in there for the night. I drop onto the bed in one of the rooms usually meant for the farmhands, but we don't have as many this year, so this room has been unoccupied. I toss and turn until five in the morning when my alarm goes off, signalling the start of a new day.

"Well, you look like shit," Garrett, one of the workers we hire every summer, comments when I surface. Ignoring his comment, I go about saddling up my horse Strider.

"Did you sleep out here?" Joe wanders into the stable with a muffin in his hand.

"Would that have anything to do with the Mercedes parked outside?" Garrett teases.

"I don't want to talk about it," I grumble. Walking past the rest of the guys, I head out to the pasture to do my rounds with the cows.

My family owns a cattle ranch. Once they only used to raise cattle for dairy, but since the economy has gone into the toilet, they've resorted to selling the cows for beef as well. I've always hated the idea of raising such beautiful creatures just to slaughter them, but fortunately we don't slaughter on-site; the cattle are only raised here and then herded to a ranch on the other side of the mountains to be culled.

I spend the entire day out in the sun working my ass off in attempt to keep my mind off of Amelia. I skip lunch so that I avoid running into her in the house. I overhear the guys talking about the hot chick helping out in the kitchen, so I'm glad I opted to starve.

"Dude, where have you been all day?" Garrett manages to corner me as I unsaddle my horse after supper.

"I've been right here." I give the horse a good rub-down once I hang up the saddle.

"No, I mean mentally." He steps in front of me so that I have no choice but to pay attention to him.

"Just a lot of my mind, I guess." I shrug before turning around to lead the horse into his stall.

"Well, you better clear it if you plan on riding tonight," Garrett warns.

"I'll be fine," I insist as I bolt the stall shut.

"We're leaving in ten," Joe calls out as he heads to the main house.

"I'm just going to change," I reply, shoving past Garrett and continuing on to my own place.

I allow the screen door to bang shut behind me so Amelia knows I'm coming, and then I jog up the steps to my room. She's laid out on my bed on the phone with somebody, but she goes quiet when I enter. I nod my head in greeting, and then grab a clean shirt from my wardrobe and my lucky belt buckle. Every time you win a rodeo, you're given a belt buckle along with whatever prize money. This is the first buckle I ever won and I've worn it for every ride since. Stuffing my wallet into my pocket, I give Amelia a wave and then run down to the guys waiting in Joe's truck.

"So Amelia's here, huh?" my brother Bonner comments once we hit the main road.

"Yeah, she showed up at my door last night." I stare out the window, watching the desert landscape float by.

"And you didn't bother to let anyone know? Mom was shocked when she walked into the house this morning unannounced. I guess she assumed you'd told everyone." Bonner fidgets with his own lucky buckle. He's a couple years younger than me, so he hasn't been riding as long; therefore, he's always more anxious than everyone else.

"He slept in the barn last night," Garrett informs my brother from the passenger seat.

"Really? I figured you'd jump at the opportunity to sleep with her." Bonner gives me a look.

"She's not like that," I spit.

"That's not what I meant. I mean actually *sleep* with her—I know you've missed her."

"Yeah, well, I'm keeping my distance," I mumble into the window, trying to ignore the looks Garrett and Joe are giving each other.

"He's been moping all day," Garrett speaks up again.

"You've got a clear head going into the arena tonight though, right?" Bonner asks, staring at me.

"Yes. Now, can we please drop it?" I pull my headphones out of my pocket and plug them into my phone. I let the music drown out the boys for the remainder of the hour-long drive to El Paso.

"There's quite the crowd tonight," Joe comments as he circles the lot, trying to find a parking space large enough for his truck. Once we finally park, we grab our gear from the bed and head into the arena to register.

"You aren't riding tonight?" Bonner asks Garrett, who remains off to the side of the registration table.

"Nah, my back is still tweaked from last week," Garrett replies, kicking at the dirt. He was always the best bull rider of the group until I started riding and stole his thunder; since then, he's been a little sulky. He took a rough ride last week getting bucked off after only two seconds resulting in a face plant. I figured he'd milk some mysterious injury to get out of being shown up by me for a while.

"There are only a dozen of us on the roster. I assumed with the amount of trucks in the lot that there'd be more," Joe comments as we head to the staging area to gear up.

"Maybe the rest of them smartened up," Bonner mutters to himself as he ties up his chaps. I step into my own chaps and zip up my vest. I'm securing the spurs on my boots when my phone vibrates in my pocket.

UNKNOWN NUMBER: You're avoiding me

The number isn't in my contacts, but I can only assume its Amelia.

DAWSON: How'd you get my number?

AMELIA: Your mom

Of course my mother wouldn't think twice about giving Amelia my number. I shove my phone back into my pocket so that I can watch Joe ride. I'm not really paying attention, though, and next thing I know Joe is bailing off at the three-second mark, receiving a score of zero.

"Shit, man, Joe really needs to work on his grip," Garrett remarks as Joe tucks and rolls away from the bull, which is being corralled back to its pen.

"Did you not see the way Florian was bucking? He was riding away from his hand, too," Bonner says, jumping to Joe's defence. I feel the vibration in my pocket and debate checking it, since I know whom it's from. However, I know she'll only keep texting until I answer so I ultimately open it up.

AMELIA: Where are you? Can we talk?

DAWSON: I'm out in El Paso with the guys.

AMELIA: When will you be home?

"Dawson, you're up!" Bonner calls from his place by the chute. I hadn't even noticed he'd moved. Tossing him my phone so that it won't be crushed in my pocket during the ride, I step up onto the gate so that I can mount.

"Left or right?" I ask, waving my hands.

"Jupiter tends to spin right." Garrett tosses me my right glove already rosined. Slipping it on, I flex my fingers to make sure it's broken in the way I like. I grip the bull rope, adjust my hat with my free hand, and then nod to the guy manning the gate to the chute.

The gate swings open and Jupiter launches himself out into the arena. Out of the corner of my eye I can see the time clock counting down my eight seconds. As predicted, Jupiter repeatedly spins right, but at the three-second mark he suddenly bucks left and I feel my ass slide so I dig in my spurs, clenching my thighs tightly around the bull's back.

Five seconds in, my thoughts drift to Amelia and how despite spending an entire day and night in the car, she still smelt like vanilla. How soft her hair felt in my fingers. The look in her eyes when I left her for Harper.

I'm jolted back to reality when Jupiter drops his front lower than I was anticipating and I'm flung forward over his head. I know I'm not coming back from this buck, so I use my free hand to push myself away from Jupiter, but my riding hand doesn't come free from the rope. I feel my arm snap as I fall towards the ground, but my fingers remain hooked under the rope. I'm left dangling from the bull as he continues to jerk about, and the bullfighters try to rein him in. Someone manages to cut the rope and I drop to the ground as Jupiter heads to his pen.

Chapter Two

AMELIA

Dawson doesn't respond to my text asking when he'll be home, so I plant myself on the front porch of the guesthouse so that I won't miss him. I know he's been dodging me, spending all day out in the fields and sleeping in the barn.

His mother has had the total opposite reaction to my return. When I walked into the kitchen this morning, Anna May dropped the bowl she was washing and let it smash in the sink as she ran up to me. I figured Dawson would have told someone I was here and word would have spread by morning, but apparently nobody knew and I caught them all off guard during breakfast. Anna May cried and hugged me for a solid ten minutes before insisting I tell her everything that's happened over the last ten years. Dawson's father Tony grunted a "hello" and left, but then he never was one for idle conversation.

I've been offered a summer position helping Anna May out, but I didn't want to accept without talking to Dawson about it first. As much as I'd love to spend the summer away from New

York in the peace and quiet of ranch life, I also don't want to step on his toes.

I was on the phone talking to my director back in New York when Dawson entered his room briefly several hours ago. I was telling Miss Leona about the possibility of my not returning for the summer intensive program. All I got from Dawson was a nod and a wave, which didn't give me much hope that he'll encourage me to stay.

The desert gets cold at night, but I'm used to New York weather, so while all the others are bundling up for the evening, I'm sitting out in my shorts—well, they aren't *my* shorts, since I hadn't brought anything with me. Anna May lent me some of her daughter's clothes.

By one in the morning, I'm growing tired and have gotten a chill, so I grab a blanket in the house and curl up in it on the porch swing. I must have fallen asleep, because I wake to the sound of tires on gravel. A glance at my phone tells me it's almost three—two hours before I know Dawson would normally be getting up. I expect the boys to pile out of the truck drunk, but instead they quietly saunter off to their living quarters with the exception of Dawson, who's standing in front of me looking tired and irritated.

"What happened?" I nod to his arm, which is casted and in a sling.

"I fell." He shrugs his other shoulder.

"You fell," I repeat dubiously.

"What do you want, Amelia?" He sighs, shifting his arm in the sling uncomfortably.

"I want you to talk to me." I stand up, letting the blanket fall to the ground.

"About what?"

"Everything: us, why you're avoiding me, why you're lying to me." I cross my arms and step down off the porch so that I'm only a foot away from him. Up close I get a better look at his arm, which is wrapped in blue fibreglass from part way up his bicep, around his elbow, and down to his hand, including his thumb, pinky, and ring finger, while his other two fingers are taped together.

"Look, I'm tired and in pain, and I just want to go to bed." Dawson goes to step around me, but I move to block his path once again.

"Not until you talk to me." I stand my ground. He drops his head back and groans. Taking a deep breath, he looks at me.

"There is no *us*. That's why I'm avoiding you, because I can't be attached to you knowing you'll be leaving. I can't go through that again."

"But I'm not leaving—or at least I don't have to if you don't want me to. Your mom offered me a job for the summer."

"Yeah, for the summer. Two months, and then what? You go back to New York and cut us all off again?"

"Can't we cross that bridge when we get there? I don't know why, but when I got in my car two days ago, my subconscious brought me here. I miss you and I need you. Please don't make me leave." I had started off angry but now it seems like I'm begging. *Great.*

"I missed you too," Dawson concedes and opens his good arm, letting me fall against him for a hug.

We head up to his room, where I change into one of his shirts and he carefully undresses, revealing the beginnings of some nasty bruises on his side. I don't want to push it so I don't say anything, instead pretending I didn't notice.

"I assume you won't be working today?" I ask as he crawls into the bed beside me.

"No, I wouldn't say I am. Dad will survive without me." He lifts his good arm so that I can slide under it and I rest my head on his chest.

"So you won't be getting up in an hour?"

"Definitely not." He laughs and I feel him wince under me.

It doesn't take long to fall asleep once the lights are out. I focus on his breathing and his heart beating beneath my ear.

This time when I wake the sun is shining in through the window and I can feel Dawson running his fingers through my hair.

"What time is it?" I mumble while rubbing the sleep from my eyes.

"Almost ten."

"Ugh, it's still early." I groan and roll away from him so I can stuff my head under the pillow.

"Early? I've been laying here awake for four hours waiting for you." Dawson laughs and lifts the pillow off my head with his good hand.

"You could have moved me," I grumble into the mattress as I remain facedown.

"You looked too peaceful. Besides, it isn't easy to do when you're lying on my one good arm." He pokes me in the side and I squirm away.

"I guess I should go help your mother prepare lunch." I sit up, squinting against the bright sunlight.

"I already texted Bonner to tell Mom you won't be in today." Dawson remains lying down.

"Well then, what am I supposed to do today?" I swing my leg over so that I'm straddling his waist.

"I thought maybe we could do something." He brushes a few stray strands of my auburn hair behind my ear.

"Have something in mind?"

"I do, actually. Now get up and get dressed." He slaps my butt, so I slide off of him and stand up.

"What am I supposed to wear?"

"Shorts and a shirt will be fine," he answers. I watch as he tries to hide his pain while getting up, but his eyes give too much away—that and the blotches of purple covering his ribs on one side.

"Hmm, mysterious," I kid, shoving my hair up into a messy bun and changing out of his shirt.

I follow Dawson down to his truck. Anna May is standing in the door of the main house, leaning against the frame and smiling at us. Bonner, on the other hand, is standing by the barn, and he's glaring at Dawson, which I don't understand since he seemed to be fine yesterday.

"What's up with Bonner?" I ask as we pull away from the house.

"What do you mean?" He takes a right once we hit the road so we are driving towards the mountains. I figured we'd be going into town.

"He didn't seem too happy that we were leaving together."

"Oh, he's just pissed at me for last night is all." Dawson shrugs.

"For you falling?"

"Yeah. So, tell me about New York." He changes the subject.

"Well, I'm part of a troupe of ballet dancers in the New York City Ballet. They offered me a spot after the spring showcase of my final year at the SAB. I've signed a contract for five years and I'm already two years in."

"What kind of shows have you done? Have you had any major roles?"

"Every Christmas we do *The Nutcracker.* Last year I was just part of the troupe, but this year I landed the part of Clara," I answer.

"That's awesome! Isn't that like the biggest part?" Dawson turns to me smiling, his blue eyes lighting up.

"It is the largest part in the sense that it has the most onstage time. However, the part everyone wants is the Sugar Plum Fairy. It's the most technical and difficult dance in the entire production. Both the solo section and the pas de deux require pure mastery."

"Did you try out for that role or are you just assigned parts based on class work?"

"The headmistress and department heads sit in on a week's worth of classes leading up to role assignment. We run through various dances in the production, and they decide who deserves what," I explain.

"So you still take classes then?" We turn off onto another dirt road that winds in through the valley.

"Well, I guess I wouldn't call them classes so much as rehearsals. We don't take them to learn, but rather to practice and to try and maintain—or ideally improve—our technique between shows."

"Is there much competition between dancers?"

"You would think so, but aside from that week leading up to when the casting list is posted, we are like one big family. I'm really close with a couple of the girls, but for the most part I'd hang out with any of them. We all want the best roles, but at the same time we respect each other's talents."

"That doesn't sound too bad, then. I was imagining like cut-throat girls who are willing to do whatever it takes to get the part they want." Dawson slows the truck to a stop on the side of the road and puts it in park.

"School was like that, but we've all signed contracts securing our places in the company, so there's less to worry about," I continue once we step out of the truck and into the hot dry air.

"That's true. So you like it?" He holds out his good hand, so I take it and we start down a trail.

"I love it—it's exactly what I had always dreamed it would be," I admit.

"Good, at least it was worth it." Dawson ducks under a branch.

"Worth what?"

"Leaving Texas."

"You mean, leaving *you*?" I ask, giving his hand a squeeze.

"Yeah." He turns back to look at me, a small smile on his face.

"How much farther?" I ask after several minutes of silence.

"Just up ahead."

We walk for another couple minutes, the only sound being our shoes crunching in the dirt. The sun is now high in the sky, beating down mercilessly and creating a sheen of sweat on the back of my neck. I'm wishing I had brought a bottle of water when Dawson pushes the branches of a bush to the side and motions for me to walk through.

"Oh my god, I had totally forgotten about this place!" I cry, rushing ahead and down the embankment to the giant rocks that border the river. We used to live here during the hot summer months as kids, swimming in the river that runs crystal clear from all the snowmelt in the mountains, or just basking in the sun on the boulders, which have been ground smooth over time. There aren't many trees in the desert, but here at the base of the mountain a small wood has grown, creating the oasis of our childhood. The rope we used to swing from is even still hanging from a tree stretching over the river.

"I thought you might have," Dawson says, easing up behind me. He had taken longer to climb down the bank since he's off balance with only one arm.

"I'd never taken that trail before so I had no idea that this was where you were leading me." I kick off my sneakers and peel off my sweaty socks.

"We were too young to drive so we always took the horses here. That route brought us slightly farther up and on the other side," Dawson replies, pointing to a break in the trees a little ways up. I remember tying the horses on by the sandy beach where they could drink and still be shaded by the trees. We'd then climb up and over the boulders to reach where we are now. The water is deeper here, almost like a pool.

"I remember," I whisper, still absorbed in the memory.

"Figured you could use some time away from people."

"Thank you." I lean my head back against his shoulder and he wraps his arm around me.

"Even I find it hot today—you must be melting."

"That would be an understatement. I'm tempted to jump in," I admit.

"Do it, I bet it would feel amazing." Dawson steps back, giving me room to strip. With just my bra and panties on I step up to the ledge, look back at him for reassurance, plug my nose, and jump.

My breath is taken away as I plunge into the freezing water. My feet touch the rocky bottom, so I push off and my head breaks through the surface. I whip my hair back with a gasp, eagerly sucking air into my lungs.

"Holy crap," I gasp, treading water.

"Cold?" Dawson laughs as he kicks off his boots and rolls up his jeans so that he can sit on the ledge and dangle his feet in the water.

"Balls, it's cold." I lean back so that I'm floating on my back.

"You don't seem to be in a hurry to get out, though." He watches me in amusement.

"Hell no, this feels incredible." I close my eyes and let my body sink under the water. I come back up when my lungs are ready to burst. Dawson is eyeing me with a distant look on his face.

"What are you thinking about?" I ask, swimming up to him and pulling myself up onto the boulder beside him.

"Just wondering what the last ten years would have been like if you'd stayed. Like what would we be now?"

"I had to leave. I couldn't stand to look at that stable anymore—not after what happened."

"I get that, and I even get why it had to be so far away, but to cut me out of your life in the process?" Dawson turns to look at me, squinting against the sun.

"I don't think I did it intentionally. I guess it was just easier to move on with my life if I wasn't still attached in some way."

"If your father hadn't died, do you think you would have come back here?"

"I don't know. Even just driving past my old place was hard. I couldn't look at it. Hearing the whickering of the horses in the stables sets me on edge."

"I'm assuming you haven't ridden a horse since?" Dawson asks, but I'm already getting lost in the memory.

My mother died ten years ago, just before my father and I moved to New York. She and I were out riding deep in the mountains when a mountain lion startled her horse. The horse reared, tossing my mom off in the process. She hit her head on a rock and was lying there unconscious. I was only fifteen and didn't know what to do. I gave her shoulders a shake in hopes of maybe waking her up; all that accomplished was her head rolling to the side, revealing smears of blood running down the rock. The seriousness of the situation hit me like a ton of bricks. She wasn't walking away from this. We had planned on going for a swim, so there were towels in a saddle-bag. I removed one of those and stuffed it under her head to hopefully stop the bleeding. Her neck was at an awkward angle, which made me want to retch, so I laid her out flat. That way it appeared she was sleeping. Checking my phone only confirmed what I already expected: no service. We were in the dead zone. I was terrified to leave her alone; after all, there is a mountain lion in the area. But she needed help. I tied her horse on by a nearby tree in an attempt to deter any other animals. Kissing my mom on the forehead, I promised her I would be right back. I spurred my horse into motion, pointing her in the direction of the ranch.

I don't remember any of the trip home, but I think I made it in record time. Bursting in through the barn doors, I startled everyone inside. My father must have read the expression on my face, because he rushed over to me.

"Mom. . . a mountain lion . . . she fell," I managed to get out between gasps. Everyone flew into a frenzy; first aid kits were grabbed, horses saddled, and doctors called. Just as everyone was ready to go, Dawson came charging in through the door. Enveloping me in a hug, he pulled my face into his chest and squeezed me so tightly I couldn't breathe. Even at sixteen he was already tall—easily a head over me. The world slowed just a tad for the first time since my mother hit the ground: that's the effect Dawson's presence has always had on me.

"We'll be right back, sweetie," my father informed me from atop his horse.

"What? No, I'm coming with you," I insist.

"You really don't need to see this." Daddy watched as the others all leave the barn one after another.

"But how else will you know where to go?" I protested.

"She has a point," Dawson spoke up.

"Come on, then," Daddy sighed.

Together, we all rode into the mountains. My mind grew fuzzier the closer we got to my mom. A part of me knows it's too late. We aren't the first to get there, since other people had left before us. When we pull up, a couple of men are kneeling beside her, feeling for a pulse. My dad practically fell off his horse, collapsing beside her in hysterics. He scooped her up and cradled her in his arms, burying his face in her hair. I hadn't noticed but I'd gotten off my own horse at some point and drawn closer to my parents. Dawson's hand reached out and wrapped around my arm, keeping me back. Spinning me around, Dawson pressed my face into his chest again so that I couldn't see my father fall apart. But he was too late; the glimpse I saw was enough. I was numb, completely numb. My brain shut off and nothing processed other than the sight of my dad clutching onto my mom's lifeless body.

That's the image circling in my head when Dawson clears his throat, bringing me back to the present.

"I don't know what I'm supposed to do now. I have no one." I can feel the tears building up.

"You have me." Dawson shifts closer to me so that he can pull me into a hug. I sniffle into his shoulder as he rubs circles on my back.

We lay out in the sun for a while, but because my red hair is accompanied by a pale complexion, I start to burn. I could tell Dawson's arm was bothering him too. He kept flexing the two taped fingers and rotating that shoulder.

It's supper time when we return to the ranch. Everyone watches as we walk into the main house together to join the family for supper. Nobody mentions us or Dawson's arm, which I thought was odd. Nobody seems fazed by the giant cast.

We head to bed not long after supper, since we hadn't gotten much sleep the night before. I fall asleep right away, but I don't think Dawson slept at all.

DAWSON

The week passes in blissful happiness, as if we are in a bubble. Amelia helps out my mother, cooking meals for the boys and doing their laundry, while I do what I can around the farm. We sleep together every night and spend every evening out on the porch talking until after the sun goes down.

"So, what's the plan for tonight?" Amelia asks after dinner on Friday.

"I'm going into town with the guys," I respond, holding the door to the guesthouse open for her.

"What do you even do?" She flops back onto the bed once we get upstairs.

"Just grab some drinks." I shrug nonchalantly.

"And you think that's a good idea, with your arm?" Amelia leans up onto her elbows so that she can observe me. I get the sense she's always analyzing my every move, as if she doesn't believe my answers at face value.

"Why wouldn't it be?"

"Because when you went out with the guys last weekend, you ended up breaking it," she deadpans.

"That was because we were being drunk and stupid." I turn to the dresser and pull out a clean shirt.

"You didn't seem drunk when you got back," she counters.

"That's because we spent a good four hours in the emergency room waiting." I won't look at her while I lie. I remain facing the wall as I change.

"So this isn't up for discussion then?"

"No, it's not. I'll be fine." I shove my phone and wallet into my pocket, kiss her on the forehead, and head down to Joe's truck.

"What'd you tell her?" Bonner asks as we pull onto the road.

"That we were going for drinks." I awkwardly put on my seatbelt with my left hand.

"And she bought that?" Garrett asks from the front.

"She seemed suspicious but didn't fight it," I answer.

"Well, nobody does that kind of damage from falling while drunk. I can't believe you lied to her about it." Bonner pats my casted arm and I grimace in pain.

"You know how she feels about horses," I say through my clenched jaw.

"Bulls aren't horses," Joe argues.

"Exactly—they're even worse. Her mom died from being thrown off a horse. How do you think Amelia will feel about me willingly being tossed off of bulls? I mean, I destroyed my arm on what I consider to be a tame ride."

"That's true, I guess." Garrett nods as my phone vibrates in my pocket.

AMELIA: I think Harper just turned up looking for you

Shit, I think. *Harper's liable to blow my cover.* I quickly shoot Harper off a text, telling her that Amelia thinks I'm out drinking with the guys and that she knows nothing about the bull riding.

HARPER: She just invited me in . . . weird?

DAWSON: I repeat: Don't say anything about the riding

HARPER: Yes Dawson, I'm not an idiot.

There aren't as many riders this week, so it doesn't take long for Bonner to be called up. Garrett is sitting out again with his back, so the both of us are left to watch Bonner and Joe ride. Bonner lasts all eight seconds and gets a relatively decent score while Joe once again gets bucked off around four seconds.

"Why does he even bother?" Garrett asks as Joe scurries away from the still spinning bull.

"Hey, I only made it to five last week."

"Yeah, but you almost always qualify, you were just distracted. Joe, on the other hand, rarely makes it to six seconds, let alone eight," Garrett mutters.

"Maybe he wants to feel included. You know the rest of the guys would give him shit for sitting out while we ride. He's never been as into it as the rest of us." I shrug.

"Whatever. When do you think you'll be back up?"

"I'll probably give it a go next week. The only reason I'm not now is because I'm still black and blue from last week. What about you?"

"Next week." Garrett nods.

"You don't want to sit out too many. You need five qualifying rides to be able to register for the tourney next month." I've already made four, so I only need one more good ride to make the cut. Joe doesn't stand a chance; he only has one qualifying ride, and there's only four more weeks until the tourney, so he'd have to have a successful ride every remaining week. Bonner has three—four, including tonight—so he only needs one more as well.

"Dude, I know. I've got three, so I just need two good rides over the next four weeks. No problem," Garrett grumbles.

"I'm just saying I wouldn't risk sitting anymore out if I were you."

"And how well, exactly, do you think you'll ride without being able to use your dominant arm?" Garrett challenges.

"I just need one of four—I'm sure I'll make it."

"If you say so." Garrett stands up to go meet Bonner and Joe, who are heading our way from the staging area.

"Nice ride," I congratulate Bonner.

"One more!" He struts over and gives me a high five.

"We'll both get to ride the tourney this year." I put my good arm around his shoulders as we walk back to the lot.

"Should be a time," Bonner agrees.

Amelia is asleep by the time we get back to the ranch, so I quietly strip down and crawl into the bed behind her. She rolls over in her sleep and cuddles into my side, mumbling something incoherent. I kiss the top of her head and fall asleep myself.

The following Friday, I straddle Thunder, slip my gloved left hand under the bull rope, and grip tightly. Lifting my casted arm into the air, I give the guy managing the gate a nod and he releases Thunder out of the chute out into the arena. I spin when he spins, counter when he bucks, and the next thing I know the buzzer rings at eight seconds and I carefully bail off to the left away from my bad arm.

"We made it!" Bonner runs up to me cheering after he also has a qualifying ride.

"We need to drink to this." Joe pats me on the back in congratulations. Garrett is sulking because he fell at two seconds, which is a record low for him.

The four of us find a nearby bar and toast to Bonner and I making the tourney. After a couple of drinks, Garrett lightens up and it ends up being a decent night. Joe stops drinking after two beers so that he's still sober enough to drive home, but the rest of us are plastered come last call at 3:00a.m.

"Now go get laid," Garrett says, shoving me towards the guesthouse once we are out of the truck.

"She's probably asleep," I slur.

"Then wake the bitch up," he laughs, stumbling towards the barn.

"Don't do anything stupid," Bonner warns, but he has a goofy smile on his face so it's hard to take him seriously.

"See y'all in the morning," I call and weave my way to the door. I try to enter the house quietly, but I must have ended up making a racket, because Amelia appears at the top of the stairs. Her arms are crossed and she doesn't look pleased.

"Hey, babe." I lean against the railing, trying to appear sober. "What are you doing up?"

"I was asleep until you came barging in, making enough noise to wake up all of Texas," she jokes, so I must not be in too much trouble.

"Sorry, we may have had a little too much to drink." I trip on a stair and fall forward. With my good arm on the railing, I end up landing on my face.

"Oh my god, Dawson." Amelia rushes down to me. "Are you okay?"

"Yeah, it'll probably kill in the morning, though." I push myself up with a grunt and she helps me up the rest of the stairs. I belly flop onto the bed, so she starts to undress me.

"Why are you covered in dust?" She shakes out my jeans, which are still dusty from bailing off the bull in the arena.

"I dunno," I mumble into the mattress. She says something in return, but I fall asleep before coming up with an answer.

Chapter Three

AMELIA

I expect some sort of explanation from Dawson the next morning, but he carries on as if last night didn't even happen. I don't know if he doesn't remember it, but I'm more confused than ever.

"Bonner, wait up!" I jog after Bonner a couple days later as he heads to the fields.

"Hey," Dawson's brother says, turning back to me.

"Can I ask you something?" I adjust the apron tied around my waist, which had come partially undone when I ran.

"Sure." Bonner shoves his hands in the pockets of his jeans.

"What happened to Dawson's arm—like, how did he break it?" I'm squinting into the sun, but I can still see the conflicted expression cloud his eyes.

"He fell." Bonner's eyes shift to the ground so he's no longer looking at me.

"Yes, that's what he said, but how? Doing what?"

"I don't really remember, exactly. We were all pretty drunk and just fooling around." Bonner shrugs, still looking away.

"Why don't I believe you?" I raise my hand to shade my eyes from the sun.

"Because I'm not giving you the answer you want to hear."

"And what answer would that be?" I probe.

"I don't know. I think you want me to admit he's up to something, but I can't do that."

"Please, Bonner, I just want to make sure he's okay," I plead.

"Does he seem okay?"

"Well, yeah, but—" I start to protest, but he cuts me off.

"Then there's nothing else for me to say." He runs his hand through his hair, making it stick up. "I have to get back to work, Dad is waiting on me." Bonner shrugs and continues on to the cow pasture.

Later that day, as everyone's returning for supper, Bonner comes storming in, letting the door bang against the wall. Dawson jogs in after him but stops when he sees me standing in the kitchen. They don't speak two words to each other for the entire meal and go their separate ways afterwards. Dawson claims not to be feeling well that evening and goes straight to bed.

The next day, the two of them act like nothing happened as they goof off around the ranch. I try dropping hints around Anna May to see if she knows anything, but she dodges all the questions, making me even more suspicious.

By Friday, I'm pissed off that everyone seems to know what's going on except for me. Why am I being kept in the dark? I decide that tonight I'm going to figure it out. After supper I pretend to be tired and crawl into the bed as Dawson changes into clothes that don't smell like manure. He kisses me on the forehead and promises he won't be out late tonight. I mumble something as if I am dozing off, and then I wait until I hear the door close downstairs. Once the guys are all in the truck, I sneak out of the house and over to my car. When they turn onto the road, I start it up and follow them, keeping a fair distance between us so that I don't draw their attention.

There's a lot of traffic on the highway to the city since it's a Friday night, so I have a hard time keeping track of where they're going. Luckily Joe's truck is a bit of a beater, so it stands out amongst all the shiny new jacked-up ones.

My heart sinks when they pull off at a rodeo arena. I try to convince myself that they only go to watch, but as I park my car I watch them take their gear from the bed of the truck. I wait until they've gone through the side entrance for the riders before I head to the main doors. I pay the admission fee and find a decent seat. I am definitely the odd one out in my dress while everyone else is wearing jeans and cowboy boots and hats.

Giving Dawson one last shot to tell me the truth, I send him a text.

> AMELIA: What bar are you guys at? I'm feeling better and might drive out to join you!

The first rider is some guy named Hunter, and he's riding a massive black bull named Napoleon. I feel like I'm going to throw up watching the poor guy get tossed off like a ragdoll at only four seconds. I make a point of concentrating on my phone for the rest of the riders instead of watching them.

> DAWSON: As much as I'd love that, I think the guys would be pretty pissed if you ruined guy's night.

He lied, point-blank. Even if he'd said he was watching the bull riders, I could have accepted that—but to completely deny me the truth?

Garrett's name is announced, so I look over at the chute to find him atop a smaller white bull with brown spots. Bonner, Joe, and Dawson are all standing on the railing alongside Garrett, helping him get situated.

I text Bonner:

AMELIA: I knew you were lying to me. Dawson fell? You forgot to mention the part about the bull.

I watch as Bonner pulls his phone out of his pocket while watching Garrett. He glances down, and his whole demeanour changes. Garrett gets bucked off around seven seconds, but Bonner doesn't even notice.

The ". . ." appears on my screen, which means he's typing. It stays that way for a while, and then disappears. I look up and notice that he's put his phone back in his pocket.

AMELIA: Don't ignore me.

I send it, but Bonner's busy helping Joe up onto the next bull. When the chute opens and Joe flies out into the arena, Bonner finally answers.

BONNER: Please don't say anything to Dawson yet. He needs a clear head to ride and if he knows you know he'll be upset and I don't want to risk him getting seriously hurt.

AMELIA: Seriously hurt?? He's riding a god-damned bull. I think he agreed to those risks a long time ago. Maybe you should have thought about that before lying to me!

Bonner looks up and scans the crowd, but he doesn't appear to see me. As badly as I want to text Dawson and yell at him, I also understand what Bonner is saying. If Dawson is upset then he won't be able to concentrate on what he's doing, and the risks of serious injury increase. Joe falls at the six-and-a-half-second mark.

Bonner is still staring at his phone, I guess debating what to say in response, but Dawson is swinging his leg over the back of a bull so he pockets the phone and hands his brother his glove.

Dawson gives the okay, and the gate swings open. The moment the bull's feet meet the dirt, my heart stops beating and my lungs stop breathing. His casted arm is in the air while he clings for dear life with the other. Around six seconds, the bull thrashes to the right away from Dawson's hand and he starts to slide, but he recovers long enough for the buzzer to ring at eight seconds. Dawson lets go of the rope and expertly leaps away from the bull, tucking and rolling until he's in the clear.

When my body decides to start functioning again, I stand up and storm back to the staging area. Garrett sees me first. He ducks his head and walks in the opposite direction, taking Joe with him. Bonner must be out on the bull, because Dawson is standing on the railing of the chute, cheering his brother on. I walk up behind him and clear my throat. Dawson turns around and his face drops when he finds me standing there.

"Amelia..." He steps down off the railing and looks down at his boots.

"Why?" is all I ask.

"Why do I ride, or why did I lie?" Dawson kicks at the ground.

"Both."

"I lied because I knew how you'd react if I told you," he starts.

"No shit. I can't believe you'd be this stupid! Do you have even the slightest idea how dangerous this sport is? You could fucking die, Dawson! It's like the most dangerous sport ever. Of all the things I thought you might be doing, this didn't even cross my mind. I guess I gave you more credit than you deserve. You know what? I don't even fucking care—go get yourself killed. I'll be in New York living a normal life like a normal human-fucking-being who cherishes their life! Because my life means something to me! Clearly you don't feel the same." I hadn't noticed, but everything has fallen silent around me. Everyone has stopped what they were doing and is gaping at the tiny girl who doesn't belong. Tears are running down my face, but I make no attempt to wipe them away as I glare at Dawson. He just stands there with his mouth hanging open. I shake my head, turn on my heel, and walk away.

When the doors to the stadium close behind me, I take off running across the lot to my car. I break all the speeding laws as I fly back to the ranch. Leaving my car running I race up to the bedroom and shove what few things I had brought with me into my purse. By the time I make it back down to my car, Anna May is waiting for me while Dawson's father is stood on the front porch.

"What's going on?" Anna May questions.

"I'm going home," I say. I toss my bag into the passenger seat and walk around to the driver's side.

"So you found out then?" Anna May leans against the side of my car so that I can't open my door.

"Only because I followed them to the stadium. How are you okay with this?"

"I wasn't at first, but I've had several years to get over it." She shrugs.

"And you just let him do it?"

"Amelia, he's twenty-six years old. What am I supposed to do? I can't ground him." She chuckles.

"You're his mother, though. He'd listen to you."

"Do you really think I haven't tried talking him out of it? I gave up when I realized it was a lost cause. He loves it—almost as much as he loves you."

"Bullshit. If he loved me, he wouldn't have lied to me."

"Would you have accepted it if he'd told you the truth when he came home that night with his arm broken?"

"No, probably not," I admit.

"Then what was he supposed to do? Lie and keep seeing you, or tell the truth and risk losing you? You didn't have to live with him after you left—he was miserable. You broke his heart, and it's taken him a very long time to get over you. You finally return, and he was so conflicted. I could see it in his eyes—he was fighting the emotions he had worked so hard to push away. You convinced him to give you another chance, so he wasn't going to turn around and tell you he rides bulls for a living. You'd have reacted the same way you are just now, and he'd lose you all over again."

"I never thought about it that way."

Headlights flash across the front of the barn as Joe's truck turns into the driveway. It pulls up alongside my still-running car and the other guys pile out, heading straight for the barn. Dawson walks around the truck and opens my car door to remove the keys from the ignition. He grabs my purse and continues on into the guesthouse. Anna May takes a step back and motions for me to follow her son.

I take my time walking up to the bedroom. Dawson is sitting on the bed massaging the two taped fingers like they're bothering him.

"Sit." He pats the bed beside him.

"I'd rather stand." I cross my arms and he sighs.

"I love you. I knew you'd be upset if you knew and I couldn't lose you. Not again. When you moved away ten years ago, it destroyed me. I didn't know who I was without you. I fell into the wrong crowd and ended up doing a lot of bad shit. Drugs, skipping school, drinking... I only barely graduated. I had planned on going to college in New York so that I could be close to you again, but that was no longer possible with my grades. I grew so depressed. I didn't think I'd ever see you again. You have no idea how much I loved you, Amelia." His eyes are becoming glossy and I think he's about to cry.

"Is this some sort of guilt trip, because—" I start, but he raises his hand to stop me.

"Then five summers ago, Garrett and Joe were hired on and we took to hanging out a fair bit. One night they were going into the city and asked if I wanted to join, so of course I went. They wouldn't let me ride that night. Garrett had been riding for years, but Joe had only ridden a couple of times, all of which ended badly, so he was hesitant to let me. I finally wore them down the following summer and I rode my first bull. It was incredible, Amelia, the rush of it all. All the noise in my head evaporated, and it was just me and the wild animal beneath me. Apparently, I'm just naturally good at it, because it wasn't long before I was getting better scores than Garrett.

"The first sixteen years of my life were spent as your best friend. That's what I was good at. I knew you like the palm of my hand. All you had to do was blink differently and I knew exactly what you were thinking. Then you were gone, and I was no longer good at anything. I didn't know what my purpose was. Being in that arena for my first tourney with the crowds cheering my name and receiving my first belt buckle for winning—nothing could top that feeling. The prize money was just the cherry on top, and I've been giving it to my parents to help bail out the ranch since the economy has gone downhill. But to be completely honest, it's not even about the winning. I just love that complete and total silence in my mind during those eight seconds. It was the only time I could really breathe."

Dawson pauses as if waiting for some sort of reaction from me, but I remain quiet.

"I know the risks I'm taking. I have to sign waivers before every ride claiming responsibility for anything that may happen. I've watched guys taken some brutal falls, breaking their necks or even being paralysed. I myself have broken my share of bones and gotten more concussions than an entire football team. But to me, it's all worth it.

"I understand why you're afraid—your mother died from falling off a horse, and that's horrible, but it was also a freak accident. She wasn't expecting that mountain lion to jump out, so she certainly wasn't prepared to be tossed. Her head happened to hit that rock just the wrong way. People get thrown from horses all the time, and for the most part, they brush themselves off and get right back in the saddle. Your mother died in a one-in-a-million chance event.

"Bull riding, on the other hand—my whole career—is built on not falling. I won't be just caught off guard like your mother was. If it gets to the point of no return where I know I'm going to fall, I know how to do so without getting hurt. There aren't any giant rocks laying around waiting for someone to hit their head, and the bullfighters are hanging around so that they can distract and corral the bull while I make it to safety. I know where to land and how to land so there's as little impact as possible. My arm broke because my hand was caught under the bull rope. I went to bail, but my glove didn't want to come free, so everything snapped. Normally that doesn't happen, but even so, it's just an arm."

I don't know if he's finished or not, so I don't say anything.

"Did that make any difference at all?" Dawson asks when it's clear I'm not going to respond.

"You may not want to lose me, but I don't want to lose you either. Except death is a little more final than moving across the country," I challenge.

"I won't die." Dawson stands up and takes one long stride towards me. He grips my shoulders and looks me straight in the eyes. "I promise you, I will never leave you."

"I'm just so scared." My bottom lip quivers as I run my fingers along his cast. "This right here is proof that anything can happen."

"I won't let anything else happen. I was distracted that night."

"Because of me." I can't meet his eyes.

"Yes, but now you know so it won't happen again." He kisses the top of my head as I lean into him. He smells like sweat and leather, which brings me comfort.

"I love you," I sniffle into his chest.

"And I love you." He tips my chin up so that he can kiss me.

I give him a nudge so he walks backwards to the bed, falling down onto it, bringing me with him. I hike up the skirt of my dress so that I can straddle him. Bending down, I gently place my lips on his. He greets me with such ferocity that it doesn't take long for things to heat up. I'm peeling off his shirt and he's lifting my dress over my head.

"You are so beautiful," he murmurs into my neck as his good hand runs down my side and cups my ass. My fingers are exploring the peaks and valleys of his abdomen while my tongue dances with his.

"I'm skinny," I whisper, pulling away slightly.

"No, you're lean—there's a difference." Dawson kisses along my collarbone. "This right here is all muscle, and it's perfection." His rough fingers trail down my legs and then back up the inside of my thighs, causing me to let out a whimper. Pushing my thong aside, his fingers play with my clitoris before entering me—one, two, and then three, stretching me out so I can take him in.

"Let me," I insist when he struggles to undo the button of his jeans with just the two fingers of his broken hand. I sit up onto my knees so that I can slide his jeans off. His boxers are quick to follow, ending up on the floor with the rest of our clothes.

He's already hard and ready to go, but I slide back so that I can take him into my mouth. His cock stands up taller, if that's even possible, as my tongue swirls around it and I gently run my teeth up its length.

"Amelia, you're going to have to stop that if you want me to come in you," Dawson warns with a grunt as I nip at the tip of his penis.

"Don't worry, I won't let you jump over the edge yet." I wink at him before letting my long auburn hair fall back down like a curtain around my face.

"Who said anything about jumping? I'm going to fall." His fingers are wrapped in my hair, tugging slightly as I tease the head of his dick with my tongue.

"Not if I have anything to say about it." I sit up and slide forward again so that his penis is up against my crotch. I grind my hips back and forth, letting my wetness provide the lubrication without him even entering me.

"Jesus, you have no idea how long I've dreamt of this." His sapphire eyes roll back, but I'm not ready to let him jump yet.

"Roll." I use the strength in my legs to turn his hips, forcing him to flip over so that he's on top.

"Your turn, is it?" Dawson grins seductively before diving face-first between my legs. I spread my knees farther apart to accommodate his broad shoulders. My head falls back against the pillow as my back begins to arch and I start to quiver.

"Not yet... together." My nails dig into his back as his mouth returns to mine. His lips are warm and salty with the wetness of me.

"You're bossy in bed." He bites at my ear lobe. "I like it." He angles his hips so that his penis teases the outside of my clitoris, causing me to release a jagged breath.

He's leaning almost all of his weight on his left arm, leaving the casted one resting against my side. The feel of the rough fibreglass on my soft skin gives me an extra boost, forcing me to claw at his back in resistance to the wave that wants to crash over me.

"Let me ride you." I peel my mouth away from his long enough to gasp.

"That'll do me in, Amelia," Dawson warns.

"That's okay, I'm ready," I whimper between laboured breaths. I wrap my arms around his shoulders and we roll once again. I shake my hair back from my face so that I can watch him as I lift up high enough for him to slide into position. I lower myself, gently at first, letting his cock slip inside of me.

"Come on, cowgirl," Dawson urges, rocking his hips against mine. I pump up and down, faster and faster, until I'm taking his entire length. My head falls back as my toes curl and back arches.

"Dawson! I'm coming." My resistance wears out as I start to quiver and the wave takes me under.

"I know, baby, I can feel it," he grunts as he releases inside of me and my whole body quakes in response.

I fall off of his lap and curl into his side. I'm oozing between my legs, but I don't have the energy to clean myself up. I nuzzle his arm until he lifts it up so that I can slide underneath and rest my cheek on his chest.

"There aren't words to describe how perfect this moment is," Dawson mumbles as he rubs circles on my upper arm with his thumb.

"If I knew this is what we were capable of, I never would have left." I play with his two good fingers as he rests his casted arm on his stomach.

"Don't joke about that." His voice takes on a more serious tone.

"About what?" I make no effort to move despite feeling him tense underneath me.

"That if we'd just fucked you would have stayed."

"I wouldn't classify what we just did as fucking. It meant more than that to me, anyway."

"So if I'd made love to you ten years ago, you wouldn't have left?" he rephrases.

"Well, no, I wasn't ready for that yet. But if I had known how you felt—"

"I thought I made it pretty clear how I felt. You were the one who chose to look the other way."

"You never outright told me, though. You flirted with all of the girls, so how was I supposed to know?"

"You were different—we were made for each other, and I thought you felt the same way."

"I don't think I wanted to see it; I wanted to live in the friendship bubble. I couldn't get hurt that way."

"So you hurt me instead by leaving."

"I'm sorry, Dawson. I'm here now and I love you. Is that not enough?"

"Of course it is." He pulls me closer and kisses the top of my head.

Chapter Four

DAWSON

The following day, I can't stop thinking about how happy I am. I've slept with a couple of other women before, but none of them even came close to what I had with Amelia. I know guys are supposed to be indifferent to it all with the primal drive to fuck everything that moves. But I take it more personally, and last night takes the cake. Ever since I hit puberty and understood the need for sex, I've wanted to experience it with Amelia. She definitely surpassed any and all expectations I had going into it. Amelia somehow manages to have both rock-solid muscle and velvety-smooth skin. Between the sounds she made and the expression on her face when she came, I don't think anyone could top it. You could say I'm eager for a repeat.

Two weeks later, Amelia's phone is blowing up as we eat a picnic lunch out in one of the back fields.

"What's up?" I ask as she types away her answer to the hundredth text.

"Nothing, my friend is just mad at me." She tosses the phone down and focuses back on her sandwich.

"Why?" I scratch at my arm, which had been released from the cast this morning. Instead of a full-arm cast including my fingers, it now starts part way up my forearm, only covering my wrist and hand. My fingers are a little stiff, but I have full movement with the exception of my wrist. I like being able to straighten my elbow again.

"We had plans to go out this weekend for my birthday, being the big twenty-five and all," she explains.

"You can still go, can't you?"

"I'm not driving all the way across the country just to get drunk with my friend." Amelia rolls her eyes.

"Don't drive then—fly."

"With what money?" I ask incredulously.

"I have more prize money then I know what to do with in this tiny town. What if Bonner and I came? We could all fly out for a weekend in the big city." I watch as she mulls it over and then sends her friend a text.

"Melanie says she's down to meet a real cowboy." She laughs. I love the sound of Amelia's laugh.

I tell Bonner later that evening to pack a bag, we're leaving tomorrow. Since the both of us already have five qualifying rides we've already made it into the tourney, so don't need this last weekend. Both Joe and Garrett, however, need this last shot to make the cut, so they won't be joining us.

"I'm kind of excited for you to see my life, you know?" Amelia chatters away as we drive to the airport on Thursday afternoon.

"Me too. There's this whole side of you I don't know."

"So this friend of yours, she's a ballerina too?" Bonner pipes up from the backseat of the car.

"Melanie majored in contemporary dance, but yes she is classically trained in ballet," Amelia answers.

"What does that mean? Majored but classically trained?" The words sound foreign in Bonner's mouth.

"I went to the SAB with the goal of becoming a ballerina, whereas Melanie studied contemporary, which is a different style of dance but has ballet roots. A lot of contemporary dancers take ballet classes just to improve their technique. We both got recruited into the New York City Ballet, but I'm a principal dancer, a lead. Melanie tends to stick in the troupe and she only really took the job to bide her time until a spot opens up elsewhere. Dancers don't like to be idle. Every day not dancing is a day our technique softens so we'll take whatever we can get until our ideal position becomes available," Amelia explains. Bonner is quiet for a moment, processing everything.

"So she's not as good as you then? Or is she just settling?"

"Neither," Amelia laughs. "Mel might not be as technical as I am in ballet but I can't move the same way she does in contemporary. It goes both ways, and in regards to her settling? NYCB is a very prestigious company that thousands of dancers apply for every year. Mel applied there as well as other places, but the company she's seeking isn't hiring yet."

"Huh." Bonner doesn't seem to be any less confused, but he stops asking questions.

We park in the long-term parking garage and haul our bags into the terminal. We pass through security without issue and board the plane. Bonner is seated by the window, and his leg is bouncing like crazy as he fidgets with just about everything.

"Can you tell he's never flown before?" I nudge Amelia, who's seated by the aisle.

"Seriously?" She looks past me to Bonner, who's paling by the second as the engine starts up.

"I haven't needed to." My brother is looking around franticly.

"Would you feel better sitting in here where you can't see out the window?" Amelia offers.

"Maybe," he grunts.

"Here, let's switch." She undoes her seatbelt and motions for me to move so that Bonner can get around me. They trade seats, and Amelia stares out the window as we start inching down the runway. "I love window seats." She doesn't take her eyes off of the horizon.

"Better?" I turn to my brother, who's gripping the armrests tightly. The plane is picking up speed and we start to lift off the tarmac.

"You've flown though, right?" Amelia asks me.

"A couple of times." I nod.

Bonner settles down a bit once we are in the air. Amelia sticks in her earbuds and zones out, so I close my eyes to nap. Next thing I know, the plane is bumping down in New York. This airport is certainly busier than the one at home, but Amelia seems to know where she's going.

"Ames!" A petite blonde runs squealing across the airport, barrelling into Amelia. They do the whole squeaky thing girls do where they jump up and down, hugging and babbling incoherent things.

Bonner and I stand back to let them do their thing. The two of them combined might make two hundred and a quarter pounds soaking wet, but they still draw the attention of anyone within hearing distance.

"So this is Dawson." Amelia introduces me after they've caught their breath. She wraps her arm around my waist and nuzzles into my side; I wasn't sure how affectionate she would be once we left the ranch, but I guess this answers that question.

"Which would make this Bonner." Melanie sizes up my brother. He and I are almost exact duplicates of each other: blonde hair, blue eyes, and well built after a lifetime of manual labour. I'm an inch or two taller, but aside from that, most people assume we are twins. I'm surprised when Melanie actually pronounces his name right. Most people pronounce it like "boner," which made for a miserable junior high experience.

"Nice to meet you, ma'am." My brother takes off his cowboy hat and bows his head in greeting. Melanie blushes bright red and giggles at his southern drawl.

"Let's go, I really want to change into my own clothes." Amelia ushers us towards the exit.

"I was going to say, there is no way you'd buy something like that," Melanie says, eyeing Amelia's outfit, which consists entirely of my sister's clothing. Tessa is a number of years older than me, and she moved out around the same time Amelia moved away. She left a lot of her older clothes behind, and my mother hasn't gotten around to getting rid of them, so when Amelia showed up with nothing to wear my mom dug through Tessa's old stuff.

"Does everyone drive fancy cars here?" Bonner mutters to me as we buckle our seatbelts in Melanie's Audi.

"Apparently," I grunt, eyeing the parking lot, which is full of similar brands. The car purrs to life and Melanie peels out of the garage. Shifting gears like a pro, she weaves in and out of the crazy traffic on the freeway.

"I like a woman who can handle a stick," Bonner jokes aloud, earning a smack from Amelia.

The buildings grow taller and the traffic slows as we approach the inner city. It takes ten times longer than it probably should have if we'd been able to drive the speed limit to get to Amelia's apartment complex because of the crowded streets. Melanie parks in the underground lot and we remove our bags from the trunk.

"Welcome back, miss." The doorman nods to Amelia as he opens the door for us.

"Thanks, Patrick. It's good to be back." She smiles and gives the old guy a peck on the cheek. We board the elevator, which climbs sixty-nine floors into the sky before opening up on the second highest level. There are only two doors: one on each side of the hall. Amelia and Melanie approach the one on the left.

The heavy wooden door swings open, revealing a scene straight from a designer magazine: floor-to-ceiling windows, dark wood flooring, white upholstery, and everything is open-concept.

Bonner and I stand in the entranceway soaking it all in, while Melanie heads straight for the kitchen and Amelia races over to the couch. She's cooing and mauling a solid black cat that looks like it hates her, but it makes no attempt to get away.

"This is Luna." Amelia pads back over to us with the cat in her arms.

"I never thought of you as much of a cat person," I comment as I cautiously pet the cat just to appease her.

"I wasn't really, but we aren't home enough to care of a dog, and the apartment just felt like it needed something. One of the girls we dance with had kittens and offered us one, so here she is two years later." She peppers the poor cat's face in kisses. Its ears are pinned back and all the signs are there that it's pissed, but it sucks it up and takes the abuse.

"So you and Melanie live together?" Bonner asks without taking his eyes off of the blonde in the kitchen.

"We do. There is no way I could afford this place on my own." Amelia laughs. "Let me give you the grand tour." She drops the cat, which takes off.

We start in the kitchen, which is decked out in stainless steel appliances, marble countertops, and mahogany cupboards with glass fronts so that you can see the perfect stacks of plates and bowls. We walk around the island to the dining area with a breakfast nook. Then there's the bar complete with fancy glasses, wine cooler, and a wall of liquor bottles.

As we step into the living room, everything opens up with a vaulted ceiling revealing bare wooden beams and twenty-foot windows with dark blue curtains pulled back. The plush white couches arch around a massive stone fireplace with a flat screen mounted above the mantle.

"There's a half bathroom through there." Amelia points to a door beside the bar. "And out here is our balcony." She pushes open a glass door built into the wall of windows and steps out onto a wide balcony overlooking the city. There's a hot tub in one corner, a BBQ and patio set in the other, and plants everywhere in between.

"This is insane." Bonner's eyes are the size of dinner plates as he walks to the railing and looks down over.

"Come on, this isn't even the best part." Amelia is already back inside.

"How?" Bonner looks at me as we re-enter the living room.

We climb a set of stairs to a loft, which has been renovated to make a mini dance studio. Wooden bars line two walls along with tall mirrors, and the floor has been replaced with the special linoleum used for dancing. There are speakers mounted in the corners and stacks of CDS alongside a stereo.

"That's Mel's room." Amelia is already making her way down the hall. She points to one door, which has Melanie's named painted in calligraphy on it.

"And this is mine." We follow her through the door across the hall. Her room is modestly sized compared to the rest of the apartment, but it's cozy. There's a four-poster canopy bed with purple duvets, and bookshelves line the walls.

"This is my bathroom. Mel has her own ensuite as well." Amelia walks up to the sink so she can fix her hair in the mirror. There's a stand-up shower and a claw-foot tub, a double sink, and I can feel the heated floor through my socks. The counter is covered in different kinds of make-up and hair appliances, all exactly as she left them a month ago.

"Ready for the best part?" She's practically bouncing up and down as she puts her hand on the door handle of the second door leading off of her room.

Her closet is literally about the same size as her bedroom. There are racks and racks of clothing, ranging from dresses and pants to skirts and tops. Shelves of heels and boots and sneakers make up one wall. The other half of the room seems to be dedicated to ballet, with piles of leotards, tights, and athletic wear. An entire section is made up of dance shoes: the fancy shoes used for ballet, both worn and brand new; regular soft ballet slippers; tap shoes; as well as a bunch of others that I don't even know what style of dance they're for.

"Amazing, right?" Amelia is seated on a pink-cushioned bench in the middle of the room beneath an honest-to-God crystal chandelier.

"Wow," is all I can think of to say as my image of her changes.

"Where did you want to go for supper, Ames?" Melanie appears behind us, leaning against Amelia's door frame.

"I've been craving that Thai place on fourteenth." Amelia rifles through a rack of sundresses before settling on a yellow strapless one.

"That sounds perfect, give me ten to change." Melanie disappears again and I hear her bedroom door close.

"Shoo, I need to get ready." Amelia pushes us out of her room and closes her own door. Bonner and I stand in the hallway, awkwardly staring at the door.

"I don't even know what to think right now," Bonner finally says, scrubbing his face and looking at me.

"Me either. This isn't the Amelia I know." I look down over the railing of the loft at the extravagance below.

"Right?" Bonner walks along the wall, looking at all the pictures hanging there. They are of both Amelia and Melanie in different costumes for different performances.

About half an hour later, Bonner and I are sitting on the couches in the living room with the cat when the girls come prancing down the stairs. Amelia's wearing the yellow sundress with strappy wedges and her auburn hair is hanging down her back in curls still wet from a shower.

"This is a different look for you." I stand up and give her a kiss.

"You just aren't used to seeing me in my natural habitat." She dramatically tosses her hair over her shoulder. Up close I can see the make-up that's been absent for the last month I've seen her.

"Come on, I'm starving." Melanie is swinging her purse over her shoulder and heading for the door.

We take a taxi to the restaurant. Amelia and Melanie chatter away to each other the entire way.

When we are seated at the restaurant, the girls already know what they are ordering, but everything on the menu is foreign to Bonner and me. We end up ordering the first thing we see, which is some sort of stir-fry. It tastes alright, but we use forks while Amelia wields her chopsticks like a pro.

Bonner and Melanie seem to hit it off, but a wall has risen between Amelia and me. Back at the apartment, Bonner follows Melanie into her room, where she can be heard giggling.

"What are you thinking about?" Amelia is sitting on her bed while I stand at the window, caught up in all the lights of the city.

"I don't know," I shrug, shoving my uncasted hand in my pocket.

"Talk to me." Amelia pats her bed.

"I've got a headache. I think I'm just going to go to sleep." I start to undress and pull the blankets back.

"Dawson." Amelia hasn't moved.

"I don't want to talk about it," I mutter as I slide into bed once I'm down to my boxers.

"And I don't want you to go to sleep upset with me." She crawls up the bed so that she's up by the pillows next to me.

"I'm not upset with you."

"Then why are you shutting me out?"

"Why did you go to Texas?" I can tell that's not what she was expecting me to say.

"I told you, I don't know. I just got in my car and drove, and for some reason it led me to you. I was upset, and I guess I still found comfort in you."

"That's all you wanted, right? You don't want a relationship or any of that bullshit. You just wanted me to distract you for a little while until you could get on with your life."

"What? Dawson, why would you say that?"

"Because look at you, Amelia! You don't belong in the south. You like dressing up and expensive things and living the fancy life. I could never make you happy. Not on a ranch in the middle of nowhere wearing cowboy boots and smelling of manure. And don't tell me to move up here, because you know this isn't me. I like wide-open spaces and the freedom to jump on a horse and ride for hours in no particular direction. I'd go crazy living in a place like this. I can feel the claustrophobia setting in already."

"Why can't I be both? Don't forget I grew up in the south. I spent more years living like you than living this life here in the city. I've been staying with you for a month now, and not once have you heard me complain about not wearing fancy clothes or not having any make-up."

"I guess. I just wasn't expecting you to be so different up here," I admit.

"Am I really different, or do I just look different? I'm still the same person. I'm just wearing a dress instead of jeans," Amelia assures.

"I'm sorry. I'm overthinking everything." I open my arm for her to hug me. She eases into my arms and I give her a squeeze.

Amelia changes into her pyjamas and turns off the light. There's a three-hour time difference so it takes me a while to fall asleep, but eventually I pass out.

Amelia and Melanie head to the studio early the next day, letting Bonner and I sleep in. Being cowboys, however, means we are used to waking up at the crack of dawn, so we are antsy and ready to explode by noon.

"I'd say we should go explore the city, but I figure we'd get lost." Bonner laughs.

"Definitely—more people live in this building than the entire city of Sierra Blanca." I flip through the channels on the TV but nothing catches my eye. Luna jumps up and starts kneading Bonner's lap.

"I hate cats," he grunts, shoving the cat away.

"I'm going to go crazy sitting here. What time did they say they'd be back?" I toss the remote on the table.

"Sometime this afternoon, I think."

"We should go see them. I'd love to see Amelia dance," I suggest.

"Do you think we could find them?" Bonner asks.

"It can't be that difficult," I reply.

We grab a cab and cross the city until we reach the New York City Ballet Center. Standing on the sidewalk looking up at the ornate building, I feel small and insignificant.

"Here goes nothing, I guess." Bonner takes a deep breath and climbs the concrete steps.

Based on the directory posted on the wall, the rehearsal studios are a couple stories up. The building is old and doesn't have an elevator, so we climb four sets of stairs before we find the right floor. The hall is packed with people in tights and leotards. I have never felt so out of place in my entire life. All of the studios have windows so you can see into them from the hall, but none of them appear to house Amelia.

We decide to ask someone, but the first few people we approach give us dirty looks and walk away. Finally, a raven-haired girl agrees to help us, although she gives me a weird look when I ask if she's seen Amelia.

"You mean Ame?" she asks, shouldering her duffel.

"I guess that's what she goes by here." I shrug and look at Bonner.

"She'd be upstairs, where the principal dancers rehearse. The troupe usually have to fight over the studios down here," she answers.

"Oh, we didn't even know there was an upstairs." Bonner laughs.

"Thanks!" I call as she continues on her way.

We go back to the stairwell and climb yet another flight of stairs. This hall is much less busy and every studio door has a name posted by it, so I guess each principal dancer gets their own space. Bonner takes one side and I walk down the other until one of us finds Amelia's name. There aren't any windows on this floor, so I hesitantly knock on the door, but the music is playing too loudly on the other side so she mustn't hear it.

I carefully open the door as not to disturb her, but she's too absorbed in the music to notice anyway. She's wearing tights, spandex shorts, and a tank top with her pointe shoes. Her hair is in a tight bun and sweat is running down her back. A song I don't recognize is playing from the speakers and she's lost in the music, spinning and twirling around the room.

"Wow," Bonner whispers beside me as we both watch in amazement. Amelia is hands down the most beautiful thing I've ever seen. Her legs seem to go on forever as she leaps despite being fairly short in stature. The muscles in her legs pop as she balances on one pointe shoe. I have no idea how she can hold herself up like that.

One song melds into another as her body continues to move with the rhythm until eventually she stops long enough to suck down an entire bottle of water. She catches sight of us in the mirror and practically jumps out of her skin.

"Holy crap." She places her hand over her heart and turns to face us. "How long have you been standing there?"

"About ten minutes or so," I reply.

"Thanks for giving me a heads-up," she jokes, tossing the empty bottle into her bag.

"We didn't want to interrupt." Bonner blushes and averts his eyes from her heaving chest.

"I think Mel should be down in studio eight if you wanted to watch," Amelia suggests as she wipes down her face and neck with a towel.

"Awesome." Bonner perks up and takes off down the hall.

"It feels so good to stretch and work my muscles again." She bends over, grabs the backs of her calves, and pulls, essentially folding herself in half.

"I bet."

"Why are you so quiet?" Amelia asks straightening back up.

"I'm just in awe, I guess."

"This is a really beautiful building. For the first few months I was here I caught myself just staring at the architecture."

"I wasn't referring to the building. There aren't words to describe how you just made me feel. Watching you dance, I finally understand why you left. I mean, you were good back in Texas, but that just now was extraordinary. If I could move like that, I'd want to show it off too."

"That wasn't even anything. I was just messing around with a new piece of music I found." She looks down at her feet where she kicks the floor with her toe.

"Modesty doesn't fit here. You can't downplay how breathtakingly beautiful your ability to move is."

"No, I just mean you should see when I'm actually following choreography. I know I'm good, I wouldn't be a principal dancer if I wasn't." I can tell Amelia isn't used to bragging about herself.

"That's more like it. A little arrogance never hurt." I take two steps to cross to where she stands, wrap my arms around her back, and kiss her.

"Can I show you something?" She peers up at me with those startlingly emerald eyes.

"Of course."

"What I'm about to show you I've never shown anyone else. It's my favourite piece I've ever choreographed, and I feel the most at home when I dance it." Amelia picks up her phone, which is plugged into the stereo. She scrolls through a list then hands me the phone. She takes her place in the centre of the room and strikes a pose. Hitting "play," I back up against the wall as the song begins.

Her eyes are closed, but her face relaxes as she finds peace within the melody. Slowly rising up onto her pointes, she lifts her right leg up into the air so it's parallel to the floor. My butt muscles hurt just thinking about attempting that. When her eyes open, she's the only one in the room.

As the intro fades and the soft lyrics begin, Amelia drops down off of pointe and becomes one with the music. Spinning again and again, her head whips around as she spots. Not once does her one leg wobble. Her leaps appear to hover in mid-air, and she lands without a sound. Legs straight, toes pointed, and arms sharp, Amelia looks exactly like the little figurines she used to collect.

The chorus picks up, allowing her more freedom. Amelia's movements soften from the strict ballet she began with. A fancy turn brings her to the floor where she rolls onto her back, arching it and clutching at her chest, demonstrating the angst the voice sings about. With a flick of her legs she's on her stomach, but a swift flip brings her back onto her feet and twirling to the centre of the room.

The tempo builds as a violin joins in the background and Amelia grows more desperate. Each kick has more force and her spins have such an intensity that I'm almost afraid she'll take off into the air. As the song draws to a close, Amelia returns to ballet and the strict lines that come with it. Arms raised above her head, shoulders dropped, and back bending just right, she falls still with the final beat of music. I'm at a loss for words. Amelia dragged me to several ballets when we were growing up, but they never had this kind of effect on me.

Even though the room has grown silent, Amelia remains in position, shoulders rising and falling with every laboured intake of air. With a long blink, she takes one last deep breath and turns to face me.

"How was that?" she asks quietly when it's evident that I have nothing to say.

"Stunning." I push away from the wall and take her into my arms.

I feel her body relax in relief as she collapses into my chest. I lift her chin with my finger and plant kisses on every inch of skin I can find. Her hands are wandering up my shirt, so I flex my abs for good measure. Hoisting her up into my arms I kneel down and lay her gently on the floor.

"Here?" she blinks up at me.

"Right now," I growl. Bending down, I trail my tongue along her collarbone while peeling back her sports bra with my fingers. My mouth finds her nipple, and Amelia sighs beneath me as I give it a nip. She grabs the bottom band of her bra and hauls it and her top over her head, exposing her sweaty breasts. I remove my own shirt and then haul off her shorts. I dig my nails into her tights and rip them away.

"I liked those," she chides with a giggle. I toss the shredded nylon to the side and flip her onto her stomach. The sweat trickles down her spine as her back arches to meet my chest when I nibble on her ear.

"Top or bottom?" I whisper into her neck as I rub my rock hard cock along her ass.

"Top of course," Amelia answers with a smirk before we roll in unison so that she's straddling me.

We fuck with more passion than we had the first time, and there's a certain ferocity in Amelia's eyes as she rides me. I'm not satisfied and I won't let myself come until she's screaming my name and gasping for air. Somehow I've ended up on top again and am squeezing her so tightly, but it only makes her cry for more. We reach the climax together as one shuddering wave rolls after another.

I'm glad there aren't any windows in this studio, and we're lucky nobody walked in on us. We take a moment to gather our senses before redressing and gathering Amelia's stuff, including what's left of her tights.

"That sure sounded like it went well," Bonner remarks when Amelia and I open the door to the hall. My brother and Melanie are sitting on a bench across the hall with smirks on their faces.

"Oh my god, you could hear us?" Amelia turns the colour of a ripe tomato.

"I'd be surprised if the whole damn building didn't hear you two," Melanie jokes, causing Bonner and I to burst out laughing at Amelia's obvious mortification.

"Oh my god," she repeats, covering her face and shaking her head. She turns towards the stairwell and scurries away from us, earning a couple chuckles from other dancers nearby.

Chapter Five

AMELIA

The four of us take Melanie's car back to the apartment. We order Chinese takeout and eat sitting in the living room while Bonner fills Mel in on the rodeo lifestyle.

"I'm going to be all bloated now. How am I supposed to fit into a dress?" Mel whines, flopping back against the couch.

"Oh shut up. You're still the size of a toothpick." I give her a smack. In fact, up until tonight, I had been concerned that she may have developed an eating disorder while I was away. She's lost a fair bit of weight, so she's even smaller than I am. However, she just ate enough Chinese for three people, so clearly I have nothing to worry about.

"Let's go get ready, then. I have a feeling it'll take me a while to find something I feel comfortable in," Mel grumbles as she pushes herself up from the couch.

"Do you need to shower or anything?" I ask Dawson before following Melanie upstairs.

"I think we're good." Dawson looks to Bonner, who just shrugs and shoves another dumpling into his mouth.

"Guys have it so easy." I give him a kiss and scamper up over the stairs.

It takes me about an hour to wash away all the sweat from ballet and to get my hair to curl just right. By the time I finish my make-up and exit the bathroom, Mel is sitting on the bench in my closet with my clothes surrounding her on the floor.

"What are you doing? You have your own closet," I laugh as I step around the piles of dresses.

"I know, but you have more, and I don't like anything I own." She pouts and crosses her arms over her still-naked chest. Growing up in the dance world has given us a certain sense of confidence. We aren't shy about our bodies; having to change quickly backstage with no time to be self-conscious about flashing everyone will do that to you. Everyone in the company has seen everybody else's naked bodies at some point.

"Well, did you want to go dress or skirt?" I ask as I pick out my own outfit. I settle on a simple black-sequined dress. It's got a halter top, clings in all the right places, and stops mid-thigh. I wear shorts underneath, because if I have to bend over, all the guys in the club would see my ass.

"If you are going dress, than I guess I will too," Mel answers. I unclip my hair so that it falls in luscious red curls down my back. I run my fingers through it to plump it up a bit.

"What about this one?" I hold up a satiny red romper. It's also a halter top, but it's looser than mine and has no back. The attached shorts aren't very long, which will show off her legs.

"How come I've never seen that before?" She jumps up and rushes over to haul on the number.

"It was right here with everything else," I shrug as she lifts her hair so that I can tie up the ribbons around her neck.

"Damn, I look hot in this." She spins around in the mirror, getting a good look at herself.

"Here," I call out before tossing her a pair of black wedged booties. Rummaging through my shoe rack, I decide on a pair of sky-high black stilettos for myself.

"Ready to go watch some jaws drop?" Mel winks at me before we descend the stairs back to the living room. The boys are still seated on the couch; however, they are wearing clean button ups instead of the plaid ones they had on this afternoon.

"Are you wearing khakis?" I ask in disbelief.

"Holy mother..." Bonner's eyes just about pop out of his head when he catches sight of us.

"Amelia…" Dawson stands up to meet me. The light blue of his shirt makes his sapphire eyes pop. He has the sleeves rolled up since it wouldn't fit over the cast so I can see his tattooed forearm.

"I was going to ask if I looked alright, but I guess that answers that question." I laugh, giving Dawson a kiss.

"Alright is an understatement." Dawson practically drools.

"You don't look too bad yourself. I don't think I've ever seen you in anything other than jeans." I go about tucking his shirt into his khakis.

"It doesn't feel right, but I'm glad I packed them. After seeing you two, I have a feeling we would have been way underdressed had we just worn jeans."

"Our Uber is here!" Mel cries when she receives the text from the driver.

"Uber?" Bonner looks to Dawson.

"It's a ridesharing service. Similar to a taxi, except they don't work for anyone," I explain.

"We don't even have cabs in Sierra Blanca," Dawson tells Melanie when she gives them a funny look.

We meet several of our friends at the club, so I introduce the boys while we wait in line outside. The girls squeal and one of them insists on pinning a pink birthday girl pin onto my dress. It takes half an hour, but eventually we make it to the front of the line where the bouncer scrutinizes my ID despite the fact I turned legal four years ago. I don't get charged cover, however, since it's my birthday.

As we walk in through the entrance, I feel Dawson tense up beside me. This is probably nothing like anything he's ever experienced before. The club is essentially a warehouse converted into the ultimate bar. The dance floor is wide open with a stage where live music would be playing, except tonight there is a DJ set up. You can go upstairs to the balconies, which overlook the dance floor; the private VIP booths are up there as well. There are three different bars: a regular bar and a shots bar downstairs, and another one upstairs.

The music is blasting with the bass vibrating through the floors. Lights are flashing enough to induce a seizure, and spotlights scan the dance floor. Dawson's hand tightens around mine as we squeeze through the crowd. Mel goes to get drinks. Of course Dawson and Bonner only get beers, but Mel brings me back some fruity concoction that's sure to give me a wicked hangover.

"Let's go dance, birthday girl!" My friend Naomi pulls at my other hand.

"Coming?" I ask Dawson, who adamantly shakes his head.

"I don't dance."

"Please," I plead, but he stands his ground.

"Bonner and I will be upstairs when you're done." He kisses my forehead and then heads towards the spiral metal staircase leading up to the loft.

Melanie joins us, as well as a couple of our other friends, as we get lost in the crowded dance floor. Arms in the air and hips swaying with the beat, I spend a good eight or nine songs dancing with the girls. Drinks keep appearing in my hand, which normally would have made me nervous in such a large club—date-rape drugging is common here. I'm working up a sweat, though, so I eagerly take the drinks and down them.

I've got a nice drunk going when I finally give in to a guy wanting to dance with me. I'd turned away several at this point. All my friends have a guy grinding on them, so I figured I might have one as well. He pulls me closer to him, so I swing my hips harder, rubbing my ass against his growing boner. He grips my waist tightly with one hand while the other one wanders up my front to my breast.

Out of nowhere the guy is ripped away, and I hear some commotion behind me. Then a pair of strong arms wraps around my waist. Breathing in the woodsy cologne, I don't need the arm cast to tell me it's Dawson. I lean my head back against his shoulder and lift my arms to weave my fingers into his hair.

"I didn't like seeing some random guy grinding on you," Dawson grumbles into my ear.

"It was all part of my master plan to get you out here with me," I giggle, arching my back so that my butt is pressing into his crotch.

A popular dance song comes on over the speakers and everyone cheers. The energy in the room picks up even more. Jumping with arms in the air, the mass of bodies grows tighter as more people join.

I feel my dress ride up as I gyrate against Dawson, whose hands are pinning me to him. I bend over to touch the floor and his hand runs up my back as I shake my ass in my signature move. I straighten back up, flicking my hair seductively and I feel his breath heavy on my neck.

I hadn't noticed Mel disappear, but she shows up at my side along with Bonner and a couple of our dance friends. I'm handed a bright pink cocktail just as the music quiets. The DJ comes over the speakers giving me a birthday shout-out; the whole club then proceeds to sing me happy birthday.

"How'd you get him to do that?" I cry when the music comes back on and everyone goes back to dancing.

"I happen to know him. I didn't know he was playing until just now, so I ran up and asked for a favour," Mel yells into my ear, since that's the only way to be heard over the music.

"Isn't he some hotshot from Seattle?" Bonner asks.

"I know people," Mel winks, and then pulls Bonner to the side and continues to grind on him.

Last call is announced around 3:00 a.m.; however, the bouncers don't start kicking people out until 3:30. We stumble out onto the sidewalk. It's raining—not that any of us seem to care. All the cabs and Ubers are busy, but when a group of guys see my birthday pin, they offer us their cab, which we gladly accept.

"Did you have a good birthday, miss?" Patrick the doorman asks as he opens the door to the apartment complex for us.

"Still having it!" I give the old man a kiss on the cheek and stumble into the elevator and up to the apartment.

Bonner and Mel have been all over each other since they got in the cab, so they fumble their way up the stairs and into Mel's bedroom without a word to Dawson and me.

"I'm such a mess." I flop back onto my bed while Dawson closes my door. He's stripping off his wet clothes. I don't think he meant it to be a striptease, but I bite my lip and eye him up anyway.

"A hot mess, maybe." He strides over to me in just his boxers and roughly grabs me by the hair, pulling my face to his. We have sloppy drunk sex before I pass out still in my dress, my hair a state and make-up smeared.

Bonner and Mel have grown quite attached to each other, and neither of them are seen all the following day. I do hear Mel squeal every once and a while though, so I know they're alive. Dawson and I spend the day lounging in bed watching movies and eating leftover Chinese. Oh, and there's sex—lots of sex.

Next thing I know, it's Sunday, and we are on the way back to Texas. This time, however, I have packed several suitcases worth of clothes and things to take with me. Mel cries as she hugs me goodbye at the airport, even though I'll be back in a month.

DAWSON 

"You should come with me," I suggest the following Friday as I get ready for the big bull riding tournament in El Paso. Bonner and I are two of the forty contestants that qualified for this round. The top five from this weekend's rounds move onto the statewide round in San Antonio a couple weeks from now.

"I don't know if I can watch you be thrown around like a ragdoll," Amelia says, picking at her nails from her spot on the bed. She's grown increasingly quiet since we got back from New York. I know she hates the idea of me riding, but she doesn't want to be the one to stop me.

"I don't even know if I'll be riding tonight. There are too many riders for one night. If that's the case, I think the guys and I will be staying out in El Paso for the night rather than having to drive back out tomorrow," I explain.

"So you won't be coming home tonight?" She looks up at me.

"Maybe not—I won't really know until we see the list, but the chances of both Bonner and I riding tonight are slim."

"I guess I'll go." Amelia reluctantly packs an overnight bag and joins us in the truck. It's a tight squeeze for the five of us, so the drive seems to take longer than usual. Especially since Amelia isn't saying much.

Amelia hardly says a word on the way to the arena and by the time we arrive I swear she's ready to snap from the anxiety. Normally I'm not overly nervous going into a ride but her stress seems to be rubbing off on me. I rub my sweaty hands on my jeans before pulling her into me for a hug. I hold her for a bit longer than necessary because I know she needs it.

"I'll let you know which number I am when we register." I kiss her forehead before we split up. Bonner and I head to the registration table while Garrett, Joe, and Amelia find seats to watch.

"You're last up tonight and I don't ride until tomorrow," Bonner informs me as he signs his waivers. I sign after him and we enter the staging area, where other guys are gearing up. I text Amelia to let her know when I'll be up and she responds with a kissy face emoji. I peek out around the bleachers and scan the audience until I see her red hair. She's sitting there, staring at her lap and chewing feverishly at her nails.

"How's she holding up?" Bonner walks up behind me and gazes out.

"She's trying to maintain a brave front, but I know she really doesn't want me to go through with this," I inform him.

Eighteen riders later, and I'm getting ready to saddle up. Harley, the guy before me, is released out into the arena and my bull is ushered into the chute. Bonner hands me my left glove since my right hand is still casted. I'm just getting settled onto the back of Orion when there are gasps from the audience and everyone starts running.

Harley has been tossed, and he's being trampled by the bull. He lays motionless in the dirt while the bullfighters work on reining in the bull. After what seems like too long, the medics finally reach Harley, who still isn't moving. I glance up at Amelia while Harley is being loaded onto a stretcher, and she's standing up, gaping at the gruesome scene below. She's ashen-faced and looks like she's about to pass out. Garrett holds onto her, keeping her upright. My heart is in my throat. There is no way this is happening.

I watch as someone tries to find a pulse. The medic shakes his head—Harley is dead. Amelia vomits and Garrett struggles to keep her standing. I've seen guys take some nasty falls before—and I mean, I've *heard* of guys who've died, but I've never personally witnessed it. Risk of death is listed on the waivers we sign before every ride, but it's amongst a hundred other things that could do wrong. Most of us brush it off. Just like how medications list side effects, which could include death, nobody actually thinks they'll die from something a doctor has prescribed. I'd taken the waivers in the same casual way. I hadn't really considered death a possibility—but now I see without a doubt, and in absolute clarity, that it is in fact a risk I've been willingly taking.

"Looks like you won't be riding tonight after all." Bonner grimly pats me on the shoulder.

"Miss, you aren't allowed back here," I hear someone say behind me. I swing my leg over and hop off the bull just in time to see Amelia stomp around the corner.

"Dawson Isaiah, you are not riding that bull." She storms up to me.

"I'm not; I've been pushed until tomorrow." I remove my glove and work on unstrapping my chaps. If I keep my own worries suppressed, then hopefully Amelia won't be so concerned.

"I mean, *ever*. You are never getting on a bull again," she cries.

"Baby," I start, but she gives me a smack, silencing me.

"Don't 'baby' me. I will walk away from you right now and never look back unless you promise me you won't compete anymore." She crosses her arms.

"Amelia..." I pull her to the side, away from all the guys staring at us.

"If you think—" She gets ready to rant, but I put my hand over her mouth.

"Listen to me for just a second," I insist. She shakes my hand away from her face, but doesn't start speaking.

"Three people die of bull-related deaths a year. Two of those three aren't even riding the bull. They're the breeders or the guys who rein in the bulls after we ride. Harley died because of the way he fell. He landed head first, which broke his neck. He was dead before the bull even stepped on him."

"Is that supposed to make me feel better?" she asks dubiously.

"Horseback riding, cheerleading, and lacrosse are considered more dangerous sports than bull riding. I promise you—Harley's death is extremely rare."

"But what if you fall like that?"

"I won't."

"How do you know, though? I'm sure he didn't mean to land on his head, either."

"No, he probably didn't, but he was a relatively new rider. I've been doing this for years. The worst I've ever gotten was my arm last month," I lie.

"It's just so scary, watching and not knowing." She leans into my chest and sniffles.

"But you do know. I'm indestructible." I kiss the top of her head and she gives me a playful smack.

"This isn't funny," she scolds.

"I wasn't joking. Aside from my arm have I ever given you evidence to the contrary?" I wait for her rebuttal but she simply furrows her brow. "Let's go," I say. I take her hand, linking my fingers with hers and lead her back out to the lot where the guys are waiting by the truck.

Nobody is really in a positive frame of mind, so we head straight for the hotel. Amelia and I book one room while the guys take a double room and Joe sleeps on the couch. Amelia curls up into my side in bed and stays that way all night. I don't sleep at all; every time I close my eyes, all I can see is Harley lying on the ground. My mind rewinds and replays the entire scene over and over again. I have managed to talk Amelia down, and as long as I make it seem like it isn't something I'm worried about, she should be alright. That does nothing to calm down the nagging fear gnawing away at my nerves, though.

"Let's try this again." Bonner hands me my glove the following night as I adjust myself on the back of Orion. The arena isn't as loud as usual, with Harley's death still dampening the mood.

"Can you see Amelia?" I ask for the hundredth time. She said she wasn't going to come because she didn't want to watch me kill myself.

"No, dude, she's not here," my brother insists. I had kind of hoped she'd show up at the last minute, but so far it seems I'm wrong.

"Ready?" the guy at the gate asks. I test my grip on the rope, stick my casted arm in the air, and give him a nod. Just as he gets ready to open the gate, I catch Amelia's red hair moving through the crowd.

The horn sounds and the chute opens, rocketing me out into the arena. I don't know if it's because she came after all or I just have a really easy bull, but I have an awesome ride. I spin when he spins and counter when he bucks. The eight-second timer rings and I bail off of what could be my best ride to date.

When I make it back into the staging area, Bonner comes running up to me and congratulates me. My score flashes on the scoreboard, bumping Dallas from the top spot. I got a 92.6, which is a full two points higher than Dallas'.

"Don't congratulate me yet. There are still twenty other riders to go, so I could be bumped off the top five," I say, warning Bonner not to jinx it.

Turns out I didn't have to worry. When the night is over, I'm still sitting in first place, and Bonner earned an 89.2, which puts him in third.

"Looks like we're going to San Antonio!" I yell as the guys race up to me afterwards.

"Dude, that was amazing!" Garrett slaps me on the back.

"And to think I was worried." Amelia leaps up so that I catch her and hold her in my arms with her legs wrapped around my waist.

"Told you." I kiss her forehead.

Chapter Six

AMELIA

A week later, Dawson and I are rolling around in bed procrastinating getting up for the day. Even though he got his cast off yesterday, the doctor didn't want him to go back to work in case he strains his wrist. That's fine by me, because it means I get more time with him.

"Your phone just vibrated," Dawson mumbles into my hair. I reach over him to grab my phone off of the bedside table.

"It's Melanie. All she said was that she's getting on a plane." I look up at him, puzzled.

"Did she mention she was going anywhere?"

"Not that I remember," I admit as I text her back, asking where she's headed.

We get up to shower and get ready for the day. Dawson may be off work, but I still have to help out Anna May. The morning passes without Melanie texting me back, so I've forgotten all about it by lunchtime, when I'm sitting out on the deck with Dawson and Bonner.

"*What*?" I squeal, reading my phone.

"Jesus, scare the crap out of us next time, why don't you?" Dawson grumbles, both guys had jumped at my sudden outburst.

"Melanie is here!" I cry, bouncing up and down.

"Where?" Bonner asks.

"At the airport in El Paso. I need to go get her!" I quickly push myself up and race for the house.

"What? I want to go!" Bonner follows Dawson, who's chasing after me.

"You have to work," Dawson tells his brother. I grab my car keys and am running back down the stairs before they even reach the house.

"We can take my truck." Dawson goes to stop me.

"My car is faster." I open the car door and hop inside as the engine purrs to life.

"I guess I'll see you when you guys get back." Bonner shoves his hands in his pockets and watches as Dawson gets in the passenger seat. I'm backing up before he even has the door closed.

"You might want to slow down." Dawson is gripping the sides of his seat as I fly down the highway.

"There aren't any cops out this far," I reply.

"That's not the point—I'd rather not die," he counters.

"So you ride bulls for a living, but a little speeding is too dangerous for you?" I look over at him.

"Eyes on the road!" he cries. I push on the gas pedal, easing my baby faster. She hugs the turns and floats over the ruts in the road.

We make it to the airport in record time. When I pull into the pickup lane, Melanie comes running out. She drops her duffel as I get out and we hug.

"What are you doing here?" I squeal.

"Amelia, we have to move," Dawson calls out the window as cars honk behind him.

"I'll tell you in the car." Mel tosses her bag in the backseat and hops in.

"Dawson, you drive so that we can talk," Mel orders him once we've pulled away from the airport.

"I can't drive stick," he admits.

"What kind of man can't drive standard?" she teases.

"The only time I ever drive anymore is if I'm coming out to El Paso. I ride my horse everywhere else," Dawson informs her.

"I can't wait to see the horses!" Melanie cries giddily. Dawson and I share a look. I haven't gone anywhere near a horse since I've been back.

Mel chatters away for the rest of the ride. We get back just in time for supper, which doesn't slow her down any. She talks everyone's ear off at the table, which seats the entire farm staff, as well as Dawson's family.

"So, this is where you grew up?" she asks later that evening as we walk around the ranch.

"Not quite. My family's ranch was next door, and it didn't have cows. We bred horses." I stick my hands out and trail them through the high grass on either side of the path.

"Can I see it?" she asks hesitantly.

"Well, someone else owns it now and I don't know them, so it'd be trespassing. But even so, I don't think I could bring myself to go back there," I admit.

"That's alright. I still get the idea of how you grew up." She nods.

"I think Bonner got the next few days off so we can go to the stream and up in the mountains and such," I say.

"Will I get to ride a horse?"

"If you want. I'm sure the guys would teach you, I just won't be there." I scuff my boots in the dirt, avoiding her eyes.

"I don't want to sound harsh, but you have to get over that at some point."

"My mother died falling off a horse. I'm not just going to jump on one as if it never happened."

"So if your mom had died in a plane crash, would you never get on a plane again?"

"Well, no, but that's different," I stutter.

"How is it different? You're way more likely to die on a plane than you are by horse."

"Thanks for making me nervous about flying," I mutter.

"You know what I mean." Melanie has stopped. When I turn around, the setting sun shines right in my eyes, so I lift my hand to shade my face as I look at her.

"I know, and I mean I have thought about it. The whole last month I've been here I considered trying it but I'm so scared."

"I'm sure Dawson would never let anything happen to you." She walks up and embraces me in a hug.

"I know, maybe." I nod, just to get her off my back.

We head back to the house, where Mel falls asleep on the couch fairly early due to the time difference.

DAWSON

Melanie hasn't stopped bugging us to let her ride a horse, so the next day Bonner and I saddle up one of the older mares and lead her out to the ring. Melanie shrieks at the sight of her and jumps up and down in excitement before we tell her to stop because she's scaring the horse.

"Sorry," she whispers. She reaches her hand out slowly and runs it down the horse's nose. "She's so pretty."

"Let me give you a hand up." Bonner rounds the horse to give Melanie a boost. She swings her leg over the saddle and sticks her feet into the stirrups.

Bonner continues to show her how to work the reins while I walk over to the edge of the ring where Amelia is standing, leaning against the fence and watching.

"I've never seen someone so excited to ride a horse before." I laugh.

"She's a city girl—you should have heard her last night while we walked around the ranch. She's never seen so much open space before. She just about broke my eardrums when we came across the field of cows."

We stand in silence for a bit watching Bonner lead the horse around in circles while Melanie sits atop trying to contain her glee.

"Is Lady still around?" Amelia speaks up after their sixth lap.

"She is," I answer simply.

"Is she still able to ride?"

"No more than a canter, but yes."

"Do you think maybe I could give her some exercise?" she asks hesitantly.

"I'll go saddle her up." I kiss her forehead and head back to the stables. Lady is an older horse; when Amelia and her family moved, we inherited a couple of their favourites that they didn't have the heart to sell. Lady was Amelia's. She was only a couple years old when Amelia left.

Lady gladly follows me out of her stable and over to the saddle rack. I talk away to her while I gear her up and she responds with flicks of her tail and the occasional whinny. I always rode the bigger broncos or geldings growing up, but I still had a soft spot for Lady. She's just so sweet, and I swear she understands you.

I lead Lady out to the ring where Melanie is watching with her mouth agape. I shake my head to Bonner, telling him to keep

Melanie quiet. I don't want to draw any attention to Amelia's decision in case she changes her mind.

"Hi, Lady." Amelia carefully approaches the horse. Lady instantly recognizes her and starts shaking her head back and forth and snorting.

"She missed you," I interpret, even though I know Amelia understands.

Amelia stands petting the horse for a while. I can tell she's trying to build up the courage to get on.

"You don't have to do this if you don't want to." I wrap my arm around her waist, pulling her into me.

"It's time." She sighs, gripping the saddle horn. Sticking her foot in the stirrup, she hauls herself up and over without any help from me. Lady doesn't budge as Amelia shifts this way and that, adjusting herself in the saddle. I hand her the reins and take a step back.

"Let's go, Lady," she leans over and whispers into the horse's ear.

Starting off at a slow walk, Lady falls into the same path Melanie's horse had made. It takes a couple of laps, but eventually Amelia gives a flick of the reins, urging Lady into a trot. The tension melts off of her as she gives into the rhythm passing Melanie and Bonner, who's still leading their horse at a walk.

"I want to go faster," Melanie whines. I can't hear it, but I see Amelia's mouth click as she signals for Lady to pick it up. Breaking into a canter, Amelia leans forward in the saddle, lifting her butt up so that she isn't being jolted by the impact. They pass Melanie a few more times before stopping alongside of me.

"Grab your horse." She smiles down at me. I waste no time in running back to the stable and saddling up my own stallion, Strider. When I get back out to the ring, Amelia is already waiting outside the fence.

"We'll be back," I call out to Bonner, who gives us a wave. I knock my foot against Strider's side, telling him to go. We start off at a slow canter out past the fields towards the mountains. When we reach a wide-open plain, I hear Amelia push Lady into a gallop and she's racing past me, kicking up dust in her wake.

Strider and I pick up our pace as well to pull up alongside Lady. Amelia looks over at me, and the pure bliss in her eyes is everything I missed. I hadn't seen her like this since before her mother died—her eyes sparkling and hair whipping behind her in waves turned orange by the sun.

Lady is old and can't keep up a gallop for long, so eventually she slows back down to a canter. I ease up on Strider without taking my eyes off of Amelia. The sun is beating down so we head for the relief of the shade. There is a brook nearby surrounded by trees, so I lead us in that direction. We hop off and tie the horses on by the water; Lady eagerly laps it up.

"I'm sorry, girl. I was just excited." Amelia pats her horse's side.

"I think she enjoyed it just as much as you did. It's been a while since anyone's tried to ride her like that." I reach my hands into the water and scoop some out to pour over Strider's rump to cool him down. He flicks his tail in appreciation.

"Thank you." Amelia encircles my waist from behind and leans her head against my back.

"For what?" I spin her around so that I can see her.

"For not pushing me—I needed to do this in my own time." She pulls at the hem of her short jean shorts to cover more of her thighs which are probably chafing.

"I know." I give her a kiss.

We saddle back up, but before we start moving, Amelia leans over and snatches my cowboy hat off my head. With an evil grin she places it on her own head, spurs Lady into a trot, then takes back off across the open desert.

Melanie had graduated to a trot without the help of Bonner by the time we return. The sun is setting, so we head behind the barn and Bonner lights a fire. We cuddle up and talk late into the night.

The next couple of days are spent riding in whichever direction Melanie points. We ride into the mountains, straight out into the desert, and even through town. Bonner surprises Mel with a pair of her own cowboy boots, which are intricately designed and have flowers engraved along the backs.

The last day before we leave for San Antonio is spent at the stream. We tie the horses on by the water upstream and hike our way over the boulders to our special spot. Amelia rolls out a blanket and plops down on it.

"Do I have to go home?" Melanie jokes, lying down beside her friend.

"You could always stay and live on the farm with me," Bonner suggests.

"Nah, I think I'd go stir-crazy after a while. I'm a city girl at heart." Melanie sighs.

Bonner and I strip down to our boxers and dive into the ice-cold water, leaving the girls to talk. Swimming farther down the river so we can't be heard over the rushing current, I tread water.

"You really like her, don't you?" I ask.

"I do. I tried not to let myself, because I knew it wouldn't work, but she's just so damn irresistible." Bonner grabs hold of a rock so that he doesn't have to swim.

"Have you given any thought to moving to the city with her?"

"You saw how I was a couple weeks ago—that is not my scene."

"But could it be? Like if you gave it time." I swim up closer to him and cling to the rock as well.

"I don't know, maybe. I mean, she's definitely worth giving it a shot."

"I've been talking to Amelia about it, so I know Melanie feels similarly. The only reason she wouldn't stay here is because of her dance career. You always said you thought about going to college, why not in New York?"

"She feels that way too? Maybe I'll look into programs offered up there," Bonner considers.

"I'm pretty sure everything is offered in a city that size. It's just a matter of finding something you can afford."

"Well, if I place during tomorrow night's competition, then I won't have to worry about it. I'll just use my prize money."

"True. Talk to her about it," I insist.

"What about you and Amelia?"

"What about us?" I hedge around answering the question.

"Have you given any thought to what happens when she leaves?"

"Of course—it's all I've thought about since she showed up on my doorstep a month ago. As much as I'd love to be with her, I'm a country boy. I would never be happy anywhere other than here." I shrug.

"And she knows you won't be following her?"

"We haven't really discussed it; it would only cause a fight. I just want to enjoy this while she's here." Bonner just nods in response to my answer. I push off of the rock and swim back upstream to the girls. Trading a look with my brother, we sneak up to the edge of the water and splash giant waves over the unsuspecting ladies.

"Dawson!" Amelia shrieks.

"Oh, you're asking for it." Melanie shakes her head. They shed their clothes and kick off their boots then jump in on top of us. Amelia takes me under, and we come up sputtering for air together.

Melanie is clinging to Bonner's back, squawking something about the water being like ice. My brother is basically pissing himself laughing at her while bending backwards forcing her further into the water. Amelia climbs up over the rocks on the other side, grips the rope swing in her hands, and then leaps off of the ledge. She cannonballs into the river, sending a wave over Melanie and Bonner.

"Oh fuck it," Melanie giggles before using Bonner's shoulders as a launch pad. She flies at Amelia, pulling her down. They start a splash war. Amelia tries to use me as a shield, so I scoop her up, toss her over my shoulder, and climb up to the rope. With the rope in one hand and Amelia squirming in the other, I swing out into the air. When she surfaces her bra is gone, and she's trying desperately to cling to me while covering up her chest.

"Where did it go?" she cries, looking around.

"I may have plucked it off while you were too busy trying to get away from me up there." I laugh.

"What the hell, Dawson!" She wraps her legs around my waist so that I'm swimming while supporting the both of us.

"Oh, come on, they haven't even noticed." I nod to Melanie and my brother, who are macking on each other. Melanie has Bonner pushed up against the rocks and they're groping each other as if they had never touched each other before.

"Gross." Amelia shakes her head with a laugh.

"I think they have the right idea." I swim over to the side where our clothes and stuff are. With Amelia still on my waist, I climb out and lay her down on the blanket. The only reason we don't have sex right there is because Bonner surfaces for air not long after. We lay in the sun until we're dried off, and then get back on our horses and head for home.

Melanie rides with Amelia in her car while the boys and I take Joe's truck to San Antonio. It's a six-hour drive, so we leave early in the morning, giving us time to grab food before the rodeo starts.

"I've never seen so many cowboys in one place." Melanie gapes at the enormous stadium, which is already almost full to capacity.

"You'd never seen any cowboys before last week."Amelia laughs.

"We better go try to find four seats together." Joe motions for the group to move.

"Good luck."Amelia gives me a kiss. She's reluctant to let go of my hand, but I reassure her for the eighth time since leaving the car that I'll be fine.

"I think they have the arena quartered so that four guys can ride at once," Bonner informs me as we sign in.

"Well, there is a shit-ton of guys here, so it'd take days otherwise." I look around the staging area, which is packed tightly with guys in chaps and cowboy hats.

"The top five from sixteen different centres are here so that's what, eighty riders?" Bonner does the mental math.

"Yeah, so four at a time is twenty rounds, same as back home." I zip up my vest and tie up my chaps.

"I'm eighth in arena two, so that's about halfway. I'm not sure which bull I'm riding, though."

"There are some big fuckers here, twice the size of what we're used to riding." I text Amelia to let her and the others know when Bonner will be riding, and that I'm fourteenth in arena four.

We pay close attention to the scoreboard as more and more riders get exceptionally high scores. There is whole different calibre of riding happening here; it's not amateur like home. When Bonner gets ready to go out, the first-place rider has a 91.6 score, and the next three are all tied at 91.5.

My brother ends up getting a bull that spins away from his hand, and he's bucked off one second shy of the buzzer. I know he's upset, but of the thirty-one other riders that have gone, fifteen of them haven't scored so he's not the only one.

"Amelia won't stop texting me. She's freaking out." I shove my phone in my pocket when Bonner returns from the medic. He has a couple bruised ribs, but he'll be fine.

"I guess me falling didn't help any." Bonner takes off his hat and runs his hand over his head.

"No, it didn't," I grumble, flexing my bad wrist.

"Melanie has been blowing up my phone since I hit the ground."

"She likes you, so of course she was worried. This is the first event she's seen, so she had no idea what to expect."

"I guess. What's up with your wrist?" My brother looks concerned.

"Nothing, it just aches from yesterday. Using it to hold onto the rope with both mine and Amelia's weight wasn't the best idea."

We remain quiet for a while as more scores are added to the board. Another sixteen fall off and nobody has beaten the first- or second-place riders yet.

"Here," Bonner says, handing me my left glove.

"No, I'm going right." I toss it back to him.

"What?" He doesn't look happy.

"It's my dominant hand," I argue.

"It was also your broken one."

"The last eight bulls have spun left. Oscar here will go right, I can feel it," I insist.

"But your grip will be compromised."

"I don't care, give me the right one." I hold out my hand while he rosins my right glove. Slipping my hand into it, I flex my fingers and my wrist before wedging it under the rope. It feels good to be using that arm again; it feels right. I lift my free hand in the air, adjust my grip once more, and then nod to the gatekeeper.

The chute opens, and Oscar bolts for the arena going full tilt. I read his stats earlier, and he weighs in at 2,100 pounds, which is just over a ton, making him the biggest I've ever ridden. I can feel the difference in the force of his bucks. Back and forth I'm repeatedly jarred as he sends his hindquarters up. The momentum of his spins—which just so happen to be to the right—is almost enough to send me flying off. I cling on for dear life as the seconds count down. Oscar gives me a run for my money since I almost fall off half a dozen times, but I keep my seat.

The buzzer sounds, and I can hear Amelia cheering over the noise of everything else. I go to bail off, but Oscar decides to veer to that side at the same time. I go to let go of the rope, but my wrist twists under Oscar's force and I feel it snap. Sliding off the side, I'm dangling with my glove still caught in the rope. Wriggling my fingers is excruciating, but I manage to get them free so I drop to the ground.

Ducking and rolling, I cover my head, but Oscar isn't done yet. I try to stay in the fetal position, but I have a bull tap dancing on my back. I can hear the bullfighters trying to rein him in, and when they get him a couple feet away, I try to stand up. I don't know what he catches sight of, but Oscar is on a mission. Heading straight for me at full speed, I drop down in attempt to go under him, but he hooks his horns under me and I'm flying.

Chapter Seven

AMELIA

I'm standing up, screaming at the top of my lungs. He did it! Dawson rode it out, and he qualified! I don't know anything about scoring, but I'm sure he did well.

"Uh-oh," I hear Garrett mumble beside me.

"What?" I turn to him. His face is white.

"He just went to bail." I look back to Dawson, who's still on the back of the bull, trying to free his hand.

"Fuck… fuck…" Joe bends over putting his face in his hands.

"I don't get it, what's happening?" I ask as panic builds.

"He's stuck," Garrett answers. When I look back Dawson is dangling from the bull, my stomach is in my throat.

"No, no, no," I cry as he drops to the ground with a *thump*. I don't want to watch, but I can't tear my eyes away as the bull tramples Dawson.

"He's up! He's moving!" Joe shouts as the bullfighters distract the monster. Dawson tries to stand up, but he stumbles and he's clutching at his arm again. He glances back just in time for the bull to haul away from the fighters.

I watch in slow motion as Dawson ducks in vain as the bull scoops him up and flings him across the arena. He's lying in a motionless heap as the bull spins around to finish the job.

"Move your leg, dude," Garrett whispers at my side, and then grimaces as the bull stomps on Dawson's outstretched leg.

It feels like forever before Oscar is finally under control and hauled away. The medics run out and an ambulance careens over the sand to the fourth corner where my boyfriend lays.

I can't feel anything, and I can't take my eyes off of the bloody scene. Garrett and Joe try to get me to move, but my feet are cemented to the ground. Melanie is screaming, but I can't hear anything other than the buzzing of my mind.

It's not until Dawson is loaded into the ambulance and taken away that sound starts to filter through. Garrett is standing directly in front of me, and he's yelling.

"He's dead," I mumble, collapsing to the ground.

"He's not dead." Joe kneels down beside me.

"There is no way he survived that," I sob.

"They wouldn't have taken him to the hospital that quickly if he wasn't alive," Garrett tries to reason, but I'm shaking my head, bawling.

"Amelia!" Joe grabs the sides of my face. "Remember Harley?"

"Amelia, do you remember Harley?" Garrett repeats. I nod.

"They didn't take him away, remember? He was dead, so the process was much slower."

"We need to get to the hospital. Dawson is waiting for us," Joe says slowly, and over-enunciates like I'm a child.

"Come on, Ames." Mel holds out her hands but I remain on the ground, unable to feel my body.

"Fuck it." Garrett throws me over his shoulder and heads for the exit. To my dismay, the other three arenas are still riding. The competition continues like nothing happened.

I don't remember getting to the hospital, but at some point the scenery changes. I'm curled up on a couch in a waiting room and Melanie is stroking my hair. Everything around me is white and sterile, and I hate it.

"I think she's back," Joe says to the others. He sits up in his chair and looks to me.

"Where is he?" I croak, my throat raw from screaming.

"In surgery." Melanie takes my hand.

"But he's alive?"

"For now," Garrett answers. I close my eyes as the onslaught of tears pour over.

"Let me." I hear Bonner's voice above me. Melanie shifts, allowing for Bonner to take her spot. He pulls me onto his lap and I curl into his chest, sobbing. I'm gasping for air when I smell it. I open my eyes to look up at Bonner, silently asking a question. He nods *yes*—he's wearing one of his brother's shirts.

Digging my fingers into the material, I burrow into the familiar scent. Bonner wraps his arms around me and rubs my back until I drift off into a fitful sleep.

"Should we wake her?" A voice filters through the darkness. I peel my eyes open, which were sealed shut by the tears. A doctor is standing in front of us, looking grim. I lean over Bonner's lap and throw up into the planter of a fake bush next to the couch.

"I don't want to know." I shake my head in denial.

"Ames, he made it through the surgery." Melanie brushes my hair out of my face.

"What?" I hiccup.

"Only family can see him right now, but I can go," Bonner says from above me.

"How is he?!" I sit up and move aside so that Bonner can get up. Everyone looks to the doctor for the answer.

"Well, he had severe internal bleeding, which was our main cause for concern when he first arrived, but we managed to stop the haemorrhaging at the cost of a kidney," he begins.

"But he'll be fine with one kidney, right?"

"Yes, but that was just the internal damage. One of the vertebrae in his neck was broken. We built a sort of scaffolding for it out of wire, but we won't know until he wakes up whether or not he'll be paralysed."

"So he won't be able to walk?"

"With a break that far up, he would be a quadriplegic: paralysed from the neck down. If he's lucky and we made the repair in time, he may have feeling in his legs, but the chances of him walking again are slim."

"But if he has feeling, why wouldn't he be able to walk?" I ask, confused.

"He sustained extreme damage to his left leg." My mind flicks back to the sight of the bull stomping on his leg. "His femur was essentially shattered. Imagine dropping a vase on the floor, all those little pieces of glass? That was his leg. Our top orthopaedic surgeon pieced together what she could, but there was no way all of those bone fragments were going back together the way they were. He's fortunate he didn't slice his femoral artery in the process, or else he would have bled out before he got here."

"Okay, so neck and leg, what else?" I pinch the bridge of my nose feeling a migraine building.

"He has several broken ribs, one of which punctured his lung. His right arm was broken in multiple places, including the still-healing fractures from before. His collarbone snapped on the same side. He did a good job of protecting his head and face, since he only has a mild concussion."

"Only a mild concussion," I deadpan.

"As far as his other injuries go, he is very fortunate that the bull didn't do any more serious damage," the doctor responds.

"That sounded to me like a whole lot of 'serious damage,'" I air quote.

"It's okay, Amelia. I'm going to see him, okay?" Bonner suggests.

"I'm coming too," I reply quickly.

"I'm sorry, but only family are allowed into the ICU," the doctor insists.

"Can't you make an exception? She's his girlfriend, and the rest of his family are six hours away." Bonner stands up.

"Fine, but just you two." The doctor nods, so I leap up and go to follow him.

We are led down a series of corridors into the ICU. This area of the hospital is quieter, and there's a chill in the air. We pass a couple of beds containing old people, and another with a bald-headed child. A couple of beds have the curtains pulled across them, so we can't see them at all.

"He isn't awake yet. We have him kept under to give his body more time to heal before he has to feel it." The doctor pulls back a curtain, revealing Dawson.

"Oh," I whimper. My knees go weak and I'm about to drop to the floor when Bonner wraps his arm around me to hold me up.

His leg is hanging from the bars over his bed in a sling. It's wrapped in plaster from his hip to his toes, with rods and various pieces of metal protruding from both his femur and his ankle. The blankets are pulled up to his chest, but I can see the tape holding his ribs together and the bandages covering the top of the incision made to fix his internal injuries, which begins at his collarbone. I can't see how far down it goes. His right arm is casted like before, with his thumb and fingers included, but this time it's strapped to his chest so that he can't move his shoulder. The cervical collar has to be the scariest, since it's a reminder that he may be paralysed.

"I'll leave you two alone with him." The doctor backs up and draws the curtain across.

"You can take the chair." Bonner motions for me to sit. I drag it to the other side of the bed so that I can hold his cast-free hand, although I still have to watch out for the IV line.

"Tell me it looks scarier than it is," I whisper.

"I'd like to say that, but I honestly don't know."

We sit in silence for a while. I continue to hold Dawson's hand, kissing it and covering it in my tears.

"I've never been in this situation before," I admit sometime later.

"No? Well I guess your mom died upon impact. What about your father?" Bonner has since grabbed a chair from an unoccupied cubicle and is sitting at Dawson's other side.

"He had a heart attack," I mumble into Dawson's hand.

"You must have seen him in the hospital then?" he asks, but I shake my head.

"He was alone, so there was nobody to call 911." I sniffle. "It was the second night of *Giselle*—Daddy never missed a show. Not one. But he wasn't in his usual seat in the audience. I knew something had to have happened."

"I'm sorry," Bonner apologizes.

"That's not even the worst part. I was mad at him for not being there, so I went to the after-party. Normally I always went out to supper with Daddy after a show, but I was spiteful so went to the party instead. When he never called me or anything, I decided to stop by his apartment..."

"Oh no." He knows where this is going.

"I found him on the bathroom floor. The coroner said he'd been dead for four hours. That means if I had gone to his place first rather than the party, I would have found him in time. He mustn't have been feeling well, so he didn't go to the show figuring I'd be by to see him after anyways." I'm shaking my head, sending tears all over the blanket.

"I am so sorry, Amelia."

"I didn't speak to anyone leading up to the funeral. I didn't even let the home have a wake for him. I figured they'd all blame me, even though there is no way they could have possibly known. The moment his casket was in the ground, I jumped in my car and drove…"

"To Dawson," Bonner finishes.

"To Dawson," I repeat, gripping his unresponsive hand tighter.

Chapter Eight

AMELIA

It's another two days before the doctors feel it's time to wake Dawson up. Bonner and I stand at the end of the bed as the sedative drip is turned off. About ten minutes pass before he starts to wake up. His left hand twitches and then balls up into a fist as he grimaces. His eyes open, but are quickly squeezed shut again as he groans and a shudder rolls through him.

"Dawson." The doctor snaps his fingers in his face. Dawson moans again and tries to fight against the blankets, arching his back and then crying out in pain.

"Dawson, my name is Dr. Pearson and I need you to look at me. We will up your morphine, but first we need to run a few tests." The doctor is speaking loudly, as if Dawson were deaf.

"I can't," he grunts through a clenched jaw.

"Up it just a drop," Dr. Pearson orders the nurse, who does as she's told.

"Dawson, I need you to look at me," he repeats.

"Get her out of here," Dawson whimpers.

"Sorry." Bonner takes me by the shoulder and ushers me out of the cubicle.

I don't think he knows I can hear him as I pace back and forth in the hall on the other side of the curtain. Listening to his yelps and cries is torture, but I have to listen to what the doctor is saying. Something about being able to move his arms and torso, so that's promising, but I don't think they established any feeling in Dawson's good leg. He can obviously feel his broken leg, but the doctor says that's probably because of the amount of stimulation the nerves are getting from the pain. Chances are he'll regain feeling in his right leg, but it's still too early to gauge whether or not he'll walk.

Before the doctor leaves, he ups Dawson's morphine supply, sending him back to sleep. Pushing the curtain aside, I stand by Bonner again, who's standing ashen-faced and staring at his brother.

"It's hard to see him like this. He's my big brother, you know?"

"I'm an only child, but I know it must be tough," I answer.

"He's always been the strong one. Nothing could take him down. Now look at him—he was supposed to be indestructible." Bonner's shoulders shudder as he tries to hold back the tears.

"Do you want to go update the others, or will I?" Melanie, Joe, and Garrett haven't left the waiting room except to sleep, and even then they take turns so that there is always someone here.

"I'll go. Melanie leaves in a couple of hours, so I'd like to spend some time with her," he gives me a squeeze then pushes past the curtain. I listen to the scuffing of his boots make their way down the corridor.

I take my seat beside Dawson once more and lean forward to rest my head on my arms on the side of his bed. His fingers are linked with mine.

I'm awoken by Dawson's hand gripping mine. My eyes flutter open to find him looking at me; they're a little foggy, but still the crystalline blue that I love.

"Do you want me to go get the doctor?" I ask, going to stand up, but his hand grips mine tighter, telling me to stay.

"No, not yet. It'll put me back to sleep, and I want to talk to you first." His voice is hoarse from lack of use.

"Talk to me about what?" I sit back down.

"Nothing in particular, I just want to make sure you're okay."

"Make sure I'm okay? You're the one lying in a hospital bed."

"I can't get the image of your face out of my mind from earlier, when I first woke up. You looked terrified, and I hate it."

"Because I was terrified. You were and probably still are in a lot of pain, and I just want to make it all go away." A stray tear trickles down my cheek. Dawson's finger wipes it away before it reaches my chin.

"I'll be alright."

"You might never walk again." I turn to his leg where it hangs suspended.

"A conversation for another time—I just want to make sure you know I'm okay. This doesn't change anything." He goes to shift and grimaces when his leg jolts.

"Don't move," I scold.

"I'm trying to look at you better. It's hard to see you with the collar keeping my head up straight like this." Dawson lifts his chin as much as the collar will allow, fighting against the resistance.

"Stop that. You don't need to look at me. You need to let your neck heal so that you won't end up paralysed."

"Sorry—I'm not used to being forced to sit still like this." He readjusts his broken arm and winces again.

"Jesus... I'm going to get the doctor." I stand up frustrated and go to find Dr. Pearson. Dawson's morphine is upped, making him drowsy, and before long he's passed out cold again.

I need to stretch my legs so I head out to the waiting room. The boys are all sitting and staring at Bonner's phone while Mel is pacing back and forth.

"What's going on?" I ask.

"Nothing." Bonner shoves his phone in his pocket.

"Mel?" I turn to my best friend knowing she'd never lie to me.

"One of the guys at the competition texted Bonner a picture of the scoreboard at the end of the tourney," Mel answers, and then shrugs at Bonner, who looks pissed.

"So?" I look to Bonner confused. He sighs and removes his phone to show me the picture. Dawson won first place with an even 94.

"Kind of ironic, isn't it?" Joe mutters.

"How did he come first?"

"He made the eight seconds. As soon as that buzzer sounds, the judges don't count anything that happens after. As far as they're concerned, he had a bad dismount. His ride, however, was near perfect," Garrett answers.

"Why wouldn't you want me to know that?"

"It's not so much you—we don't want Dawson to find out," Bonner clarifies.

"But he can't ride, so what difference would it make? Wouldn't it make him feel better knowing his ride was still the best?"

"Amelia, he qualified to go to nationals, which are almost three months away. Think about that for a moment."

"But he can't ride anymore."

"In three months time, he won't be in those casts anymore. You know Dawson—if he knows he's qualified, then he will go regardless of whether or not he should."

"So you're saying if he knows he came first, then he will rush his recovery so that he can go?"

"Yes," Garrett nods.

"He's not that stupid. If he happens to fall, he'd be paralysed for sure. It's so much more dangerous now, and he won't be in the same physical shape as he was this time," I argue.

"Amelia, you've been gone the last ten years. Dawson is a proud guy, and unless we tie him to that bed, he's going to go."

"But what if the doctor tells him not to?"

"If he can sit on a bull, he can ride the bull. In his eyes, anyway," Joe supplies.

"I won't let him." I cross my arms stubbornly.

"Look, Ames, I have to head to the airport now." Mel walks up behind me and lays her hand on my shoulder. I spin around and wrap my arms around her.

"Do you have to go?" I mumble into her hair.

"I already extended my trip a few days. I can't afford to miss any more rehearsal with the show coming up in a couple of weeks."

"I know—I could just use a little more estrogen around here." I motion to the guys who force grim smiles.

"You'll be home in a couple of weeks, anyway. I'll see you then." Mel kisses my cheek.

"Maybe." I pull away and look at the floor.

"What do you mean, maybe? You're coming home, right?" Her voice takes on a whole different tone.

"Dawson is going to need me," I start.

"You are not throwing away a decade of training and a career you've dreamed of forever for a guy."

"But he isn't just a guy. I love him, Mel." The boys have grown silent behind us.

"Will you still love him when he's in a wheelchair and not the ripped cowboy you were drawn to in the first place?"

"I can't believe you'd even say that. The last time I saw him, he was a scrawny teenager. I didn't know he looked like he does until I showed up at his door a couple months ago. Yet I was still drawn to him—I love him for him," I answer.

"Fine. Well, I guess I'll see you around then. I just really hope to find you in our apartment two weeks from now." Mel shoulders her purse and turns for the exit. Bonner follows after her, I assume so that they can say good-bye in private. I slump down into a nearby chair and rest my elbows on my knees with my head in my hands.

Dawson is moved to a regular room the next day so the guys can visit and we aren't limited to two people at a time. He spends most of the time asleep, though, because of the pain medication.

Anna May manages to get away from the ranch a couple days later and makes the six-hour drive to the hospital. I had asked her to bring my bags with her, so I check into a hotel across the road from the hospital and have my first real shower in six days. Dawson's father Tony had to stay behind to man the ranch, but I know Dawson understands his absence.

When I return to Dawson's room later that day, I'm clean and in a better mood, but he quickly squashes that. The physical therapist and Bonner are attempting to move Dawson from his bed to the chair, as was suggested by the doctor. Dr. Pearson figures it would be good to get him up and moving now that he's regained feeling in his good leg.

"No, Amelia, get out," Dawson barks at me when I step foot into the room. The therapist is holding him up by the waist while Bonner supports him under his good arm. Dawson is red-faced, grimacing and clearly in a lot of pain.

"I want to help. What can I do?" I take a step further into the room.

"Leave," Dawson grunts as he makes another hop in the direction of the chair with his casted leg dragging behind him.

"No." I stand my ground. I watch him mumble something to Bonner, who stops and helps him turn as much as the collar with allow.

"Please," Dawson pleads.

"But why?" I'm baffled.

"Amelia." Bonner shoots me a look as his brother turns his focus back on the chair.

"Well, let me know when I'm allowed back, I guess." I retreat to the hall where I lean against the wall, trying to figure out what just happened.

"He's a proud man," Anna May says, appearing beside me.

"I just want to help," I whisper, holding in the tears.

"And he knows that, sweetie, but he also doesn't want you to see him like that, either," she reasons.

"Like what? I don't see him any differently?"

"Tell him that."

DAWSON

I've been in the hospital almost two weeks and the doctor has been weaning me off of the morphine, so I'm becoming increasingly frustrated with the pain. My mother, Garrett, and Joe all had to return to the ranch, so only Bonner and Amelia are left to occupy me. I'm losing my mind.

"It's a gorgeous day. Did you want to go outside?" Amelia suggests as I sit in bed scrolling through Facebook on my phone, like I do just about all day every day.

"How do you suppose I do that?" I don't take my eyes off of the phone.

"We could get you in a wheelchair."

"I'm not having you push me around in a wheelchair like a cripple," I snap.

"Fine, it was just a suggestion," she mutters. A notification pops up on my screen. When I open it, I find a link to a news article about me—about how I came first in the latest rodeo and should be headed to nationals in a couple of months, but due to my injuries, I've had to forfeit.

"What's this?" I hold up my phone to Amelia.

"Oh," is all she says before dropping her gaze to her lap.

"You knew I came first?" I accuse.

"Bonner told me not to tell you."

"So everyone knows? Nobody thought to mention to me that I won?" My voice is rising as my temper boils.

"They thought you'd want to go to nationals, so it'd be better if you just didn't know," Amelia stutters.

"Damn right I want to go to nationals. Who decided to make this decision for me?" I motion to the article and how it states I've forfeited.

"I think they interviewed Bonner last week." Her eyes grow wide as I become visibly upset.

"Its two and a half months away. I'll be out of this bullshit by then," I shout, giving my leg cast a smack.

"Dawson, don't do that," Amelia cries.

"Don't fucking tell me what I can and can't do!" I whip my phone at the wall, where it shatters and falls to the ground in pieces.

"I'm sorry," she starts, but I'm flinging the blankets back and sliding my leg off the side of the bed. "What are you doing?" She jumps up to stop me.

"I'm walking. What does it look like? I have two months to get back into shape. I'm not letting a bit of plaster stop me." I push myself up off the bed so that I'm standing on my good leg.

"What has gotten into you? Back on that first day that we spoke, you said that nothing has changed, but you aren't the same guy I fell in love with." Amelia's crying.

"Clearly, I'm not the same guy." I spin around to face her, knocking my broken leg off the bed frame. I curse, but continue on anyway. "I used to be the strong, bull-riding cowboy. Now I'm confined to a bed, broken and weak."

"I don't care that you don't ride bulls anymore—that's not what I loved about you." She reaches out to touch me, but I yank my arm backwards. The momentum pulls me backwards, so I stumble, stepping back onto my casted leg. Not a good idea. A shock of pain shoots up my leg, and I drop to the floor.

"Dawson!" Amelia rushes over to help me up.

"Don't." I hold out my good arm to stop her. You'd swear I'd slapped her by the look on her face.

"What is wrong with you?"

"I don't need your help," I grunt, trying to stand up.

"Clearly," she replies saucily.

"Just leave, Amelia," I spit.

"You really want me to leave?"

"Is that not what I just said?"

"And you're going to ride in nationals?"

"Yes. The only way I'm forfeiting is if I'm dead."

"Alright." She takes a step back, shaking her head. "I won't stand around and watch you kill yourself, Dawson. I'm heading back to New York first thing in the morning. Text me... or don't." She spins on her heel and stomps out of the room.

"Dude, what did you say to Amelia?" Bonner asks as he appears in the doorway. He's watching her, so doesn't notice me at first. "Dawson? What the fuck are you doing on the floor?"

"Don't just stand there," I grumble. My brother races around the bed and struggles to lift me up onto the bed. I had forty pounds on him before all the plaster, so I can only imagine how much I weigh now.

"What just happened in here?" Bonner takes a step back once I'm seated in the bed. I massage my leg, even though I can't feel it through the cast.

"I fucked up, man." I sigh and lean back against the pillow. My neck is killing me from the fall.

"Care to elaborate?"

"I told her to leave and that I didn't need her help."

"Amelia wouldn't lose her cool over that. You've been telling her that for two weeks now."

"I may have also said I was going to ride in nationals," I supply.

"What the fuck? Why?" Bonner looks genuinely perplexed.

"Because I am?"

"Like fuck you are."

"Why does everyone seem to think they can control me?" My anger is burbling up inside me again.

"Because your last ride landed you here, and you probably won't be able to walk, little alone sit atop a bull."

"I have two months to prepare; the casts will be gone and I'll get back into shape," I insist.

"This isn't like riding a bike, Dawson. You can work out all you want, but if your leg doesn't want to walk, there's nothing more you can do."

"I don't need to walk. I just have to sit there."

"You and I both know there's more to it than that. You need a lot of leg strength to hold yourself on top of that beast."

"I'm not having this conversation anymore. I'm going to prove you all wrong." I roll onto my good side so that I'm facing away from my brother. Bonner curses under his breath and I listen to him walk away.

Towards the end of my third week in the hospital, the doctor's deem my internal injuries healed enough so that I can be transferred to the hospital in El Paso. The only reason I need to stay in the hospital at all is because there isn't even a clinic in Sierra Blanca, and I need physical therapy every day, so it's just easier than driving the hour to and from.

I'm transported by ambulance the seven hours across the state to the new hospital. This one is significantly smaller, but that doesn't make much of a difference to me. At this point I can stand up and hop to the chair on my own. I would be able to use crutches if it weren't for my arm and shoulder, so until they're better, I'm stuck in a wheelchair.

I've only been set up in my new room for an hour when there's a knock on my door. My hopes are dashed when I find Harper standing there.

"Don't look so disappointed," she kids.

"Sorry, I thought you might have been someone else." I turn my attention back to the television.

"She hasn't even texted you?" Harper wanders into the room and takes a seat in the chair beside my bed.

"Nope."

"That sucks."

"It wasn't going to last, anyway," I mutter.

"She really loved you. I saw you guys out and about together like at the rodeos and such, and it radiated off of her," Harper babbles.

"I don't want to talk about her."

"That's fine by me. Do you mind if I just hang out here for a bit?" Harper asks. I shrug my response, so we sit together and watch old *Family Guy* reruns for two hours.

Chapter Nine

AMELIA

Melanie doesn't say anything when she comes home to find me sitting in the living room. She simply hugs me and then asks if I want to grab dinner.

I missed the first couple days of classes, so I have to work extra hard to make up for it. I throw myself into the choreography and push myself until I'm too tired to think about anything other than how tired I am.

When the casting list goes up for *The Nutcracker*, which we perform every December, I'm not expecting to be cast as the Sugar Plum Fairy. I figured I'd be a snowflake or something minor—sort of as a punishment for bailing during the middle of the spring show, and then arriving late to the fall season.

But sure enough, beside the Sugar Plum Fairy role is my name: "Amelia Claiborne." The other girls all congratulate me and offer to go out for drinks, but I politely decline. Melanie is nowhere to be found for some reason, so I make note of her roles so that I can tell her when I see her.

"What did you get?" Patrick the doorman asks me as I arrive home later that evening.

"Sugarplum," I grin.

"I knew it!" The old man cries and gives me a strong hug.

"Thanks, Patrick." I give him a kiss on the cheek and continue to the elevator.

I unlock the door to the apartment and toss my keys on the table. As I round the corner to the living room, I'm startled to find Mel sitting on the couch with Bonner. I stop dead in my tracks and my heart does a little dance. It's been six weeks since the accident—would Dawson be able to travel?

"Oh, crap. Ames, I'm sorry, I didn't think you'd be home this early." Mel jumps up quickly and flattens out her skirt.

"It's okay. I didn't know we were expecting anyone." I adjust my bag on my shoulder.

"Bonner is here looking at colleges. I would have told you he was dropping by, but I figured you'd be out celebrating," Mel stutters.

"I wasn't really in the mood," I reply, watching Bonner, who won't make eye contact with me.

"Oh well, he was just leaving." Mel gives Bonner's foot a kick.

"Why are you guys being so awkward?"

"After everything that happened with Dawson, we didn't know how you'd react to me being here," Bonner finally speaks up.

"You didn't push me away. He did," I reply.

"I guess. So Sugar Plum Fairy, huh?" Bonner shifts on the couch so that he's facing me better.

"How'd you know?" I laugh, looking to Mel.

"I knew this morning who got what. That's why I didn't bother going to the posting," she explains.

"Ah, well, yeah, I'm excited." I grin.

"Now that we've got the awkwardness out of the way, I'm going to go grab a shower so we can go for supper," Mel tells

Bonner. He nods and gives her a kiss before she runs up over the stairs. I take a seat beside him and we sit in silence for a moment.

"How is he?" I finally get up the nerve to ask.

"Emotionally or physically?"

"Both, I guess."

"Well, he's home now. His arm cast was shortened so he can straighten his arm out, allowing him to use crutches. He has physical therapy like every other day, and he's getting stronger, but he still has a long road ahead of him. He goes back out to San Antonio next month to get the rods and everything removed from his leg. He'll still have the leg cast for like a month after that, so he isn't happy, but whatever," Bonner answers.

"What about his neck?"

"He still has to wear the collar for a while yet but the doctors say his spine is healing nicely."

"Good." I nod and we fall into silence again.

"He really regrets saying what he did."

"He could have texted me. I've been waiting for some sort of apology, but I haven't gotten a word," I respond.

"He's too proud," Bonner admits.

"His pride will get him killed," I answer.

"We haven't been able to talk him out of riding yet. We're just counting on the doctor keeping him casted until it's too late."

"He's so stubborn."

"He is."

I dive headfirst into rehearsals for *The Nutcracker*. I need to be perfect. I spend just about every day and every night at the studio. That's where I am one evening in the middle of November. I'm switching pointe shoes for the third time today when footsteps enter my studio.

"Those are some nasty-looking feet," a male voice sounds from above me. I look up to find Damian, who plays the Nutcracker, standing over me.

"They are pretty gross, aren't they?" I laugh, and then go about applying Band-Aids to certain blisters.

"I guess that's what happens when you work as hard as you do," Damian comments.

"I think every ballerina's feet look like this at this point—no pun intended." I laugh, and his deep, throaty chuckle joins in.

"I've been meaning to ask, but I haven't had the courage. Do you think you'd go for a drink with me some time?"

"Oh!" My head jerks up. "I'm not really sure a relationship is what I need right now."

"Who said anything about a relationship? I'm just asking for a drink right now. Baby steps." He smiles.

"I'm not sure." I stand up and work on stretching out my feet.

"Would this have anything to do with a certain southern guy?" He asks, causing me to blush. How does he know about Dawson?

"Um, no, I'm just so busy with rehearsals and whatnot."

"I'm in the same boat, remember? You have no worries about me dealing with your busy schedule, because I'm right there with you." He's not letting up.

"I guess, sure. Why not?" I laugh.

"Awesome! How does tomorrow night sound?"

"Works for me. Pick me up at eight? I'll text you my address." He agrees and leaves me to practice.

Apparently, Mel was in on this, because she keeps prying when I get home that evening, asking if anything interesting happened today. She then insists on dressing me for the date. I think she's more excited than I am.

The date is pretty unremarkable. We have trouble talking about anything other than ballet. It's the only thing we have in common, so somehow every conversation circles back to it. Damian is a really sweet guy, though, so I give him the benefit of the doubt and we go on several more dates leading up to the show.

We have sex a couple of times, but it doesn't feel right. I try to tell myself it has nothing to do with Dawson, but I keep finding myself comparing the two men. Male ballet dancers are rarely more than six feet, because any taller than that makes it difficult to pair. Damian sits at about five foot eight, whereas Dawson is a hulking six foot four, and he has a good hundred pounds of pure muscle on Damian. I mean yes, Damian, is fit—he has to be, to lift me all the time—but that ruggedness isn't there. I try to turn that part of my mind off, but I think Damian can tell I'm not really putting my all into our relationship. I don't know what I'm holding out for.

DAWSON

The national bull-riding tournament comes and goes and my leg is still in a cast, so I begrudgingly forfeit. I'm not happy about it, but Harper does a good job of keeping me occupied. She's over every day and drives me to and from therapy, since I can't drive myself. I don't know what she thinks we are, but I'm not going to bring it up unless she does.

"You decent?" Bonner knocks on the door to my bedroom, which is now in the main house since I can't handle stairs.

"Yeah," I grunt, turning down my music.

"Mel is performing in *The Nutcracker* in a couple of weeks. She sent me a couple of comp tickets, so I was thinking about flying up to New York for that weekend."

"So?"

"I was thinking maybe you'd like to come," he offers.

"And why would you think that?"

"Because Amelia is the Sugar Plum Fairy," my brother answers.

"I'm with Harper now."

"Are you, though? Anybody with eyes can tell you aren't happy."

"Would you be happy being in a cast and neck brace for almost four months?" I snap.

"You know that's not what I meant."

"I don't even think I can fly."

"Ask your doctor. Just think about it, alright? I won't mention it to the other guys until you tell me for sure you won't come."

"Whatever." I put my headphones back on and turn up the music.

Amelia is at the front of my mind again, and she's all I can think about as I ask Dr. Pearson if I'm okay to fly. He says I am. I tell Bonner I'll take that second ticket and I pack my bag for New York.

"Fuck, I forgot that it's winter here." I'm rifling through my suitcase, trying to find something to wear to the recital.

"It's fancy anyway, so your only real option is a suit," Bonner remarks as he buttons up his own white dress shirt.

"I don't know if my dress pants will fit over the cast." At home, it's basically always summer, so I've gotten away with just wearing shorts, which is about the only thing that will fit over the cast.

It's a tight fit, but we end up squeezing the pants over the bulky cast. We had to make a small slit along the seam at the bottom so they'd be wide enough around the ankle, but with a black sock over my foot, you can't really tell. I wear a dress shoe on my good foot and wear the same light blue button up I wore the last time I was here.

"Need a hand?" Bonner asks as I fumble with my tie.

"How'd you get so good at tying ties?" I mutter as my brother takes over knotting my tie for me. It's just a simple skinny black tie that I keep for funerals.

"I watched a lot of YouTube videos before I came to visit Mel during the fall. I knew I'd be visiting colleges, so I figured a tie would look the most professional." He sticks his tongue out in concentration as he creates the perfect knot, but leaves it hanging loose around the stupid neck brace I still have to wear.

"Little brother is growing up," I tease. He punches me in the shoulder and then grabs his suit jacket.

We hail a cab in front of the hotel even though the opera house isn't far. My shoulders will be sore tonight from all the crutching, so why walk farther than we have to? I'm having difficulty manoeuvring through the crowd on my crutches, so we stop to the side to let the people thin out a bit.

"Holy shit, dude." Bonner elbows me and points to the ticket booth. Based on the seats that were assigned to our complimentary tickets, we would have had to pay three hundred dollars a pop.

"People really pay that much?" I'm baffled.

"Apparently." Bonner shakes his head in disbelief.

There's a break in the flow of people, so we make our way down to the orchestra seating and squeeze into the row. We are a couple seats in, so a few people have to get up to make room for me to crutch in. I better not have to pee at any point.

As the lights dim, I'm conscious of the crackling the paper makes that wrap up the flowers we bought for the girls. Apparently it was a wise decision on Bonner's part, since a lot of the people seated around us also have bouquets for their dancers.

The curtain rises to random people dressed as maids and such wandering about the stage. Kids come out followed by people in fancy dresses. They appear to be having some sort of party. The woman playing Clara flits about the stage, and I try to picture Amelia playing this part last year. The party ends, Clara falls asleep, and then some guy in tights prances out and fights off some mice with his toy soldier pals. Clara is whisked off to wonderland or wherever and the curtain drops for intermission.

A lot of people get up to stretch their legs, and I really wish I could join them because my leg is killing me being squished up like this. I'm a tall guy, so not being about to straighten out my legs for this long would bother me anyway, but toss in the cast—which I have to stick awkwardly to the side, since it doesn't fit under the seat in front of me—and it's even worse. Unfortunately, I think it would be too much work to get back to lobby, so I stay seated while Bonner texts Melanie. Apparently, she was one of the party guests, but I didn't notice.

This time when the curtain rises, ballerinas are scattered about the stage in all white. They flutter about like snowflakes, and I pick out Melanie right away. Clara and tights guy return and they meet a whole slew of people. Melanie returns several times as different characters from a Russian to a Spanish dancer.

I don't know how, but somehow I know she's coming up next. Something about the air in the room changes as Amelia dances out onto the stage on her pointes. She's in a light purple suit with a massive tutu, and she has a tiara atop her perfect red bun. All the other dancers fall still around her. I know it's all part of the show for them to watch her, but I feel like there's more behind it.

Amelia's solo is flawless. I know nothing about ballet, so I don't think I would notice a mistake anyway, but I can tell by the way she carries herself that she's proud. She's delicate yet strong at the same time, and every step is perfectly synchronized to the music.

Sooner than I'd like, the music melds into a different piece and tights guy saunters over to join her. I instantly hate him. He's lifting her and touching her in ways I no longer can. The longer they dance together, the more jealous I get. He lifts her for one final lift, and I watch Amelia's eyes scan the audience. I know she's probably looking for her father. This is the first show she's done since he's died. I don't know if his usual seat was around where I'm sitting, but her eyes find mine easily. My breath hitches, but she makes no sign that she recognized me. But how couldn't she, when I have this god-awful neck brace? It stands out, so there's no way she missed it.

My mind is occupied for the remainder of the performance with the images of Amelia dancing with that guy. Next thing I know, the curtain is dropping and everyone is clapping. The curtain lifts for the last time, and group by group, the dancers file out for their curtsies. Melanie comes out towards the end with a couple of the other girls I noticed that danced multiple roles.

Amelia skips out alone and bows in the centre of the stage; the audience is standing at this point. Tights guy comes next, followed by Clara. Once everyone is onstage, tights guy holds his hand out to Amelia, who takes it, and he pulls her up front with the two leads. Then right there, in front of thousands of people, he plants a kiss on her lips. And to my horror, she accepts it. Cheers erupt amongst the clapping, and I want to be sick.

AMELIA

As soon as the curtain lowers after our final bows I spin around, grab Mel by the arm and haul her into one of the wings.

"Why didn't you tell me he was coming?" I yell at her.

"I didn't know he was coming!"

"Bullshit, they were seated in your comp seats," I accuse.

"I sent Bonner two tickets assuming he'd bring Garrett or someone. Never in a million years did I think Dawson would come. I mean, based on everything Bonner has told me, I thought Dawson was seeing some Harper chick." As soon as the words leave her mouth, she regrets it. I can tell by the look in her eyes that she never wanted me to know.

"That's fine, I don't care. I'm with Damian anyway. It just would have been nice to know he'd be in the audience, rather than spotting him while I'm in the middle of a lift. I totally spaced out for a second. It's a good thing Damian didn't drop me," I huff, trying to play off that I don't care. *Is Dawson really with Harper*?

"I'm sorry, Ames. Bonner didn't tell me until yesterday that Dawson was coming. I kind of just hoped you'd never see him so you'd never know, you know?"

"Yeah, it's fine. Let's go collect our bouquets from our many adoring fans." I plaster on my show smile and make for my dressing room. I find Damian waiting for me there with a massive bouquet of roses, all different colours and sizes like he'd bought the entire florist out.

"There she is." He walks up to me and kisses me again. I was mortified when he kissed me onstage, but what was I supposed to do? I couldn't very well push him away in front of everyone.

"Are these for me?" I pretend to be surprised when really I want to toss them in the trash and go find Dawson.

"Of course—only the best for my Sugar Plum Princess," he grins, clearly pleased with himself.

"We should get out there—we're supposed to be signing autographs and such." I quickly change into sweats and fix my make-up.

"I'm already ready. You're the one that ran off after curtain call and disappeared for ten minutes." He means it as a joke, but I flinch. Thankfully, he doesn't catch it.

We walk out into the lobby holding hands, which makes me uncomfortable, since I have a feeling Dawson will be waiting for me. The lobby is packed tight with people, so it takes ages to get to the table where Damian, Gina (the girl that plays Clara), and I will be signing autographs. We then proceed to spend an hour taking pictures with little girls and signing pointe shoes. I always love this part—all the tiny ballerinas telling me they want to be me when they grow up. Because I was that kid; I remember when Mom took me to my first show, which was *Cinderella* in San Antonio.

My hand is cramping and I think my face is stuck smiling by the time the line ends. Damian leans back against his chair with a sigh and closes his eyes. I'm about to text Mel and ask where she is when I spot Bonner across the room. Standing beside Bonner is his brother. Dawson's eyes are boring into me, but I can't read him.

I push away from the table while Damian is talking to Gina and walk up to Mel, who's clinging to Bonner's side.

"Woah, Amelia! You were so good!" Bonner cries when he notices me standing there.

"Thanks, I didn't have nearly as much to learn as Mel, though." I give my friend a hug.

"Oh shut up, you were perfect," Mel gushes. "Oh, look at the flowers Bonner gave me!" She sifts through the bundles of flowers to find a specific bouquet, eventually settling on a cluster of lilies. White lilies have always been Mel's favourite. I wonder if Bonner knew that.

"You were flawless," Dawson says. He hands me my own bouquet of flowers. I had left all the others at the autograph table so his are the only ones I'm holding. They are a simple dozen red roses, yet they're perfect. They aren't flashy and trying too hard like the ones Damian gave me, proving how well Dawson knows me.

"Thank you, they're gorgeous." I lift them to my nose, breathing in the sweet scent.

"No more gorgeous than you," he states, causing me to blush.

"How are you?" I notice he's leaning heavily on his crutches, and the mask he has on to disguise the pain is fading. Dawson opens his mouth to answer when Damian sidles up beside me and wraps his arm around my waist, kissing my temple.

"There you are. I turned around and you were gone." He laughs.

"Sorry, I came over to see Mel and a couple of friends from home." My gaze flicks to Dawson, hoping that didn't hurt him as much as it hurt me to say.

"Oh wow, what happened to you?" Damian addresses Dawson, sizing up the cast and neck brace.

"Just an accident a few months back," Dawson replies. As soon as he begins to speak, Damian turns to look at me. He picked up on the southern accent and knows who this is and what he means to me.

"That's unfortunate—ready to go get ready for the party, babe?" Damian keeps his eyes on me and his grip tightens, showing a possessiveness that I don't like.

"Will you be coming back to our place for the after-party?" I ask Dawson, shrugging Damian's arm off of my shoulder.

"Bonner is, but I think I might just head back to the hotel. My leg is bothering me," he answers, and I feel Damian loosen up beside me. I hadn't realized how tense he was. Was he going to punch Dawson if he said yes?

"Alright, well don't be a stranger," I insist as Damian tries to lead me away. The look on Dawson's face is enough to crush any high I had coming off of the dance show.

I take my time packing up my dressing room with the goal that by the time I get back to my apartment, it's already full of people. Damian was harping on me the whole way about being slow, but I don't want to spend any time alone with him at my place.

Patrick hands me a single red rose when I walk into the building, which makes me want to cry. I give him an extra strong hug in thanks while Damian just rolls his eyes.

We ride up the elevator in silence; however, when the doors chime open on my floor, we are hit with chaos. People are spilling out of my apartment into the hall, and the music is blasting from inside. When I walk in the door, the place erupts in cheers and applause. I say my thanks and retreat to my bedroom.

I manage to lose Damian before I get up there, so I close the door, shutting out the noise. I toss my bag onto the bed and haul out my phone.

> AMELIA: Thanks for the flowers and thank you for coming.

My thumb hesitates before hitting send, but I ultimately go ahead with it just as there's a knock on my door.

"Babe, are you in there?" Damian calls over the music.

"I'll be right out!" I quickly change out of my sweats into a pair of skin tight, black skinny jeans and a lacy green top that brings out my eyes. Ripping the elastic from my bun sends a spray of bobby pins everywhere. My hair falls down around my shoulders in waves.

"Ame, what are you doing in here?" Damian's voice has grown inpatient as he opens my bedroom door and walks in.

"I was changing. Jesus, chill out." I poke my head out of the bathroom where I'm washing off my stage make-up and replacing it with my regular stuff.

"We are all waiting on you down there."

"The party seemed to be in full swing without me. I'm sure they'll survive another ten minutes," I remark, sliding my phone out of my back pocket when it vibrates.

> DAWSON: You're welcome. You deserve so much more than that though. You truly were the most incredible thing I've ever seen. It was even worth dealing with that new boyfriend of yours.

"Who are you texting? Everyone you know is here." Damian stalks into my bathroom, so I shove my phone back in my pocket before replying.

"Not everyone felt welcome," I snap, taking a step backwards.

"What the hell is that supposed to mean?" He takes two steps forward so that he's basically on top of me.

"Ames, you in here?" Mel wanders into my bedroom, making Damian back off. She's my best friend, though, so she can read the look on my face and knows I need to get out.

"Sorry, I just had to change." I make my voice sound more light-hearted than I feel.

"Let's go, shots are waiting!" She loops her arm through mine and drags me off downstairs.

There's a tray full of tequila shots on the counter for all of the cast members. They encircle the island in my kitchen and each grab one. We toast to another amazing production, and then toss back the amber liquid.

Mel already has a nice buzz going and she's hanging off of Bonner's arm. I take my phone out and send Dawson my response.

> AMELIA: I'm sorry you had to see him kiss me like that. If I knew you were coming I would have avoided it.
>
> DAWSON: No, it's my own fault. I don't know what I was thinking showing up like that. I'm just glad you're happy.

His reply is almost instantaneous.

The room feels like it's closing in around me and I struggle to get a full breath. I push through the clusters of people out onto the balcony, where it's slightly less crowded. The air is crisp with winter frost, which feels glorious on my clammy skin. I lean against the railing until I catch my breath.

> AMELIA: I wish you showing up had happened earlier. You are about a month too late.

"What's going on with you tonight?" Damian appears behind me, causing me to jump. I stash my phone in my bra, but it's too late. "Who are you texting?"

"Nobody, let's go back inside." I go to head to the door, but Damian grabs hold of my arm a little too tightly.

"It's that cowboy, isn't it?" He seems almost resigned to the fact that it is.

"Dawson." I nod. Damian closes his eyes and rubs his hands through his hair.

"I'd be kidding myself to believe I stand a chance against that guy. I knew you were still hung up on him when I first asked you out." His voice has softened.

"I didn't know he was coming tonight. I didn't even think he could fly in his condition," I insist.

"You love him, don't you?"

"I don't know," I answer honestly.

"Well, I'll give you the space to figure that out. You know where to find me if it turns out you don't. I'll be waiting." Damian kisses the top of my head before leaving me by myself.

I take a deep breath and remove my phone with shaking hands.

> DAWSON: I would have been here two months ago if I could have travelled.

Racing back indoors, I climb onto the back of a chair so that I can see over the crowd. Scanning the room, I spot Mel, which means Bonner will be close by.

"Where are you staying?" I shout over the noise once I reach him.

"What? I thought I was staying here tonight?" Bonner's eyes are glazed over.

"No, I mean which hotel did you book at?" I clarify. Realization dawns on him and he nods.

"The Holiday Inn over on sixth, Room 312." He gives my shoulder a squeeze.

Chapter Ten

DAWSON

I hadn't anticipated Amelia texting me when I got back to the hotel. It just drives the knife deeper into my gut. Changing out of my suit, I lie in bed and flick on the TV, not that I'm paying attention to whatever is on.

> AMELIA: I wish you showing up had happened earlier. You are about a month too late.

That text makes me want to hurl my phone over the balcony. *Fuck this . . .*

> DAWSON: I would have been here two months ago if I could have travelled.

If that doesn't tell her everything she needs to know, then screw her.

The screen remains blank as she makes no effort to reply. She's probably too busy partying with her douchebag boyfriend. I toss my phone on the bedside table and roll over to go to sleep.

I'm in that weird state of being asleep, but aware when there's a knock on the door. I curse Bonner for forgetting his room key, grab my crutches, and hobble over to the door. Amelia is standing there, looking effortlessly pristine as always. Neither of us says anything for a minute.

"Can I come in?" She finally breaks the silence.

"I guess." I shuffle backwards, giving her space to walk past me. She makes it to the centre of the room, and then spins around to face me. Her mouth opens to say something, but then closes again.

"I don't know what to do." Her voice cracks as she breaks down into sobs. I close the distance between us and pull her into my bare chest.

"I am so sorry, Amelia, for everything," I mumble into her hair. She shifts and I wobble momentarily, losing balance on my one leg.

"Sorry, did you need to sit? Is your leg bothering you?" She looks up to me with her eyes still watering. She runs her finger under her eyes to wipe away the tears and in turn smears her mascara.

"My leg is fine. I only said that as an out so I wouldn't have to go watch you and tights all night. But yes, we can sit." I hop over to the bed and lay my crutches on the floor.

"Are you sure? You looked like you were in pain." She sniffles as she sits down beside me.

"I was, but my leg was the least of my worries at the time. I get the cast off next week, anyway."

"Oh, well, that's good. Gosh, it seems like you've had it forever." She runs her index finger along the blue fibreglass.

"Tell me about it. It shouldn't have taken this long to heal, but they took the rods out too soon. Apparently my femur is stubborn and a few of the fractures shifted, so I had to have everything reset again. They're leaving a couple pins in there for extra support."

"Like forever?"

"Yeah, it's going to be a pain for airport security," I joke, earning a chuckle from Amelia.

"I'm not with Damian, by the way."

"It sure looked like he thought so," I counter.

"He did at the time, but we've since talked."

"And you broke up with him?"

"Not exactly—he gave me an out telling me to decide. He'll be waiting for me if I don't pick you." Her brutal honesty hurts a bit. I would have felt better thinking she'd dumped his pathetic ass.

"Did you pick me?"

"I haven't decided yet." Amelia fidgets with a ring on her middle finger.

"Oh. Then what are you doing here?"

"I love you, Dawson. I really do, but you also terrify me. My mother died, and then my father died, and then you almost die. It's just too much, you know? After my dad's funeral, I drove to you because you had always been my safe place. You kept me afloat after my mom's accident. But who do I turn to if you were to die? That's all I kept thinking about when you were lying in that hospital bed. Who will keep me going, if not you?

"I understand your love for bull riding, because I share the same passion for ballet. It's my outlet and my reprieve from the chaos that can be my mind. I've even continued to do recitals after injuries, even though doctors advised against it, but it was never a matter of life and death. And I didn't have someone I loved asking me to stop. I was ready to take a year off and stay with you in Texas, help you through your recovery. I was ready to drop everything to be with you because you needed it, but you threw that back in my face and insisted on competing in a competition that had almost just cost you your life. I asked you not to, and you essentially told me to go to hell. That hurt, Dawson."

"I know. I've beaten myself up every day over that for the last four months. I knew what I was saying when I said it, and I guess part of me was mad at you for being right. You told me not to ride and I did it anyway. Then you had to witness me suffer through the consequences. I hated you seeing me in pain, so I don't know if it was my subconscious pushing you away, but I have regretted that day every moment since."

"I wish that were enough," she whispers.

"Is this you choosing Damian?" I ask against my better judgment.

"Damian is safe—he's a ballet dancer, for god's sake." She chuckles. "I always know what to expect and I don't have to make any sacrifices for him."

I nod and sigh in resignation.

"But he isn't you," she finishes.

When I look at her, she gives me a small smile, and then lifts her leg and slides it over my lap so that she's straddling me.

"I missed these eyes," Amelia admits, brushing a stray piece of hair from my forehead.

"I missed all of you." I cup her butt in my palms and she giggles.

"I wish you didn't have all of this on the go." She motions to my neck brace. I slide my hands out from under her, unclip the collar, and then toss is across the bed.

"Problem solved." I give her a kiss.

"But what if I hurt you?" She pulls away nervously.

"It's more of a precaution at this point—I'll be fine." I return to kissing her. Amelia gives in and kisses me back. Draping her arms gingerly around my neck, she intertwines her fingers through my hair and inches her body closer so that our chests are touching. I lean back so that I'm lying down, taking her with me.

"Not tonight," she murmurs.

"Why not? I promise you won't hurt me," I assure.

"That's not it." Amelia's fingers trail back and forth along my cast.

"If it's my leg, the cast will be gone in a week. I agree it would be nice to do this cast-free for once," I try to joke.

"No, the thing is, I don't think I'll be seeing you in a week," she admits quietly.

"Well, no, but soon enough."

"Dawson, I'm staying in New York. I'm not choosing Damian, but I'm not ready to choose you either. I need to spend some time just focusing on me." Amelia slides off my lap and pulls her knees up to her chest.

"Oh."

"I shouldn't have to be dependent on someone for my happiness. I need to learn to be happy on my own, to grieve my father on my own."

"That's understandable."

"I don't want you to wait for me. You are such an amazing guy and you deserve the world. I don't know if I'll ever be stable enough to be that for you. I know you're going to say I'm full of shit and that I'm more than good enough for you, but that's just who you are. Go back to Texas and date Harper or whoever. Don't hold out for me."

"What are you getting on with, Amelia? I love you and I've been dying without you. I only dated Harper to fill the void you left when you walked away."

"Just promise me if some nice girl comes along and asks you out, you'll say yes." The expression on her face is so sincere it hurts.

"I promise, but I also promise that if you show up in Texas six months from now, I'll drop everything and everyone for you." I give her a kiss on the forehead.

"You fly back in the morning, don't you?"

"Yep," I answer with a grim nod.

"Can we pretend the last six months never happened, just for tonight?"

"Of course." I haul back the covers and crawl underneath them. Holding up my arm, Amelia slides in under and curves into my side, fitting perfectly. I try to stay awake for as long as possible, relishing the moment, but eventually I drift off to her soft snores.

When I wake up, light is filtering through the curtains and the space next to me is empty. Amelia is gone.

AMELIA

I cry the whole way back to my building. I sneak into the apartment, passing by several people passed out on the couches. I knock on Mel's door and then creep inside.

"Ames?" Mel squints through the darkness of her room. Bonner is snoring beside her. I cross the room without a word and climb into the bed next to her. "Oh, sweetie," she coos into my hair when I let out a sob. She holds me and rubs my back until I calm down enough to tell her what happened.

The New York City Ballet performs *The Nutcracker* for two more weeks leading up to Christmas. Mel goes to her parents' in Boston for the holidays and I accompany her, since I don't have anywhere else to go.

Damian jumps on me the moment we return, but when I tell him I'm not interested, he backs off. Several other guys approach me when word gets around that I'm single, but I ignore all their advances.

Rehearsals pick back up in January when it's announced we'll be performing *A Midsummer Night's Dream*. I'm given the role of Hermia, which is one of two lead female characters. The corps de ballet spend two months perfecting the show, and then we hit the big stage at the end of March. Bonner is seated in the audience but Dawson doesn't join him, which I appreciate.

Mel flies down to Sierra Blanca for spring break, but I stay behind and take a two-week technical intensive program.

Swan Lake is chosen to be our spring production, and for some reason the competition heats up amongst the principal dancers over the lead roles. I had broken two toes during the program I took over spring break, so my dancing isn't as seamless as I'd like, which makes me nervous. I have to take a week off of pointe while they heal, which hurts my chances for the lead.

When the cast list is posted, I expect to see my name beside the cygnets, which are the main swan companions of Odette. One of the other principals, Lindsay, has been getting a lot of attention from the directors ever since her performance as the other lead, Helena, in *A Midsummer Night's Dream*. But Lindsay's name isn't alongside Odette; mine is.

Mel and I go for dinner to celebrate and spend the evening out at the club. I dance with several guys, but take none of them home with me.

Damian was cast as Prince Siegfried, which is Odette's love interest, so we end up spending a lot of rehearsal time together. Thankfully, he doesn't push anything. According to Mel, he's messing around with one of the troupe girls, so that takes the heat off of me.

Two months fly by and the year anniversary of my father's death is fast approaching. June 28th happens to fall a couple days before the opening of *Swan Lake*, so hopefully I'll be past the grief by then.

The day actually ends up being unremarkable. I go to rehearsal, eat supper with Mel, dance on my own for a while, and then head home. Bonner is there, since he's made a habit of being at the opening night of all of Mel's shows. The three of us have a couple drinks and then head to bed.

Odette has always been a dream role of mine. It's not just the fact that it's a lead, but it's an incredibly difficult performance to master. The arms, which mimic swan wings, are so intricately choreographed, right down to finger movements. It's a challenge, making the finished result that much more satisfying.

The opening night was a little painful as I look out at the audience and don't see my father's face. There have been numerous shows since he died, but for some reason this one is different; maybe because it's so close to his death, or it could be the time of year that triggers stronger emotions.

After the final curtain call, I retreat to my dressing room and collapse in the chair at my make-up table. *Holy crap*—I'm riding such a high. There's a knock at the door, which I assume to be Mel, but when I get up to answer it there is a lady in a suit on the other side.

"Good evening, Miss Claiborne. My name is Ashley Baer and I'm with the American Ballet Theatre Company." She holds out her hand and I shake it.

"Oh, hi. I didn't know you were watching tonight," I admit, flustered.

"No, and we try to keep it that way. We get a more honest performance when dancers don't know they're being scouted," Ashley explains.

"Scouted? Sorry—did you want to come in?" I open the door wider and motion inside.

"Thank you—yes, scouted. I'm here to offer you a principal position in our company. We are just finishing off our spring production, much like you are now; however, we are going on tour soon. I think you would make an excellent addition to our cast."

"I'm afraid I've signed a five-year contract with NYCB. This is just the end of my third year," I apologize.

"You get the summers off though, correct?" I nod. "ABT will be spending the summer touring Europe. Join us and return to NYCB in the fall. Although I have dealt with their contracts for other dancers I've recruited, and if I'm not mistaken you aren't required to commit to five consecutive years. I do believe you're allowed to take a gap year or two."

"Really? I didn't exactly read it all. I was too excited just to be offered a position." I blush.

"Well, is ABT something you'd be interested in? Again, you can take the summer and tour with us. If it's not for you, then no harm, no foul," Ashley offers.

"Will I have to sign a contract similar to NYCB's committing to so many years?"

"Yes, but that's more for you than for us. We aren't allowed to fire you or let you go until those years are up. You, however, are allowed to leave whenever you want—as long as it's not mid-performance, of course." The woman laughs. "You could work both simultaneously if you think you could handle that much. We are based out of New Jersey, so as long as show nights don't overlap, you could potentially dance for both companies while we're stateside."

"Wow, yes, I am definitely interested!"

"Here is my card. Give me a call next week to confirm. I already have your email, so I'll send you the rehearsal schedule."

She hands me a business card, shakes my hand again, and leaves me shocked.

I race out into the hall and down to the troupe dressing rooms to find Mel. She's facing away from me talking to another dancer when I run up to her, squealing. I wrap my arms around her and jump up and down.

"Jesus, Ames, what got into you?" Mel laughs and manages to turn around.

"*Guess what*?"

"I haven't the faintest idea."

"ABT just offered me a principal position in their company!" I shriek. Mel's eyes bug out, and she's yelling and leaping about with me.

"Seriously, though, holy crap." Mel stops to catch her breath.

"They're touring Europe this summer, so the manager suggested I join them to get a feel for the company, and then if I like it the position is mine. She's even willing to work around my contract here, so I can do both!"

"That is beyond amazing, Ames. You deserved this. I've never seen you dance the way you did tonight—you've worked your freaking ass off this year." She shakes her head in disbelief.

"Let's go celebrate!" I cry before beelining it back to my dressing room to finish changing.

A bunch of the other dancers with NYCB join us at the club, where I don't spend a dime since everyone keeps insisting on buying me drinks. By the time I get back to the apartment, I'm plastered. Stumbling into my room, I flop onto my bed face-first.

I take out my phone to plug it in to charge and notice I have a missed text from Dawson.

> DAWSON: I heard you got a once in a lifetime opportunity to dance with some prestigious company abroad. Can't say I'm surprised. I always knew you'd do incredible things. Just thought I'd congratulate you and wish you all the best. Go be the star you were born to be. Love you.

The screen blurs towards the end of the text as tears bubble up—happy tears to end the perfect night.

Chapter Eleven

AMELIA

I finish out the spring season with NYCB as Odette while learning the choreography to the role I'll be dancing with ABT. We'll be performing *Sleeping Beauty* and I play Fauna, one of the fairies, so I don my green leotard and tutu with my little pointed hat.

As of the second week of July, I'm on a plane to Europe. Mel insisted I send her a postcard from every city, so I stocked up on international stamps. Our first stop is France, where I get to practice the French I took as an elective in college. Our shows are at night, so aside from the hour or so where we go over staging, all of our days are free. This postcard is of the Eiffel Tower, obviously.

During the middle of July, we travel through Belgium (I get a postcard of some fancy cathedral). We eat some waffles, of course. We go to the Netherlands as well—making many jokes about each other's "Nether Regions"—and take a tour of the Anne Frank House.

The last week of July is spent in Germany, where I get to see the Berlin Wall and taste real German ale. We spend an extra day after our last performance so that we can ski the Alps. Mel's postcard is of the Neuschwanstein Castle, which looks like something from a fairytale.

With August comes Poland and its medieval architecture and Renaissance fairs. We take turns trying to pronounce the crazy names of places while on the tour bus. We visit the remnants of the Auschwitz Concentration Camp, which is one of the most darkly monumental places I've ever been. The air changes as soon as you walk under the gate, almost like you can feel the death in the air.

After our last show in Poland, I get a message from Mel asking me to Skype her when I get the chance. I respond that we are on the way back to the hotel and that I'll be calling in about an hour.

"Hey! How's my worldly best friend?" Mel asks after her face appears on the screen of the computer.

"Tired, but a good tired, you know?"

"I would say you are—a month straight of dancing and travelling will do that to you," she comments.

"It's so crazy. I've been in five countries in the last four weeks." I shake my head.

"Speaking of which, why did I not get a postcard from the Netherlands?"

"We were only there a few days and we were so busy that I forgot," I admit.

"Unacceptable," she jokes.

"So what did you want to talk about?"

"Bonner got his acceptance in the mail today for the community college in Queens."

"That's awesome!" I'm glad my best friend won't have to do the whole long-distance relationship thing anymore. It was becoming expensive.

"The only thing is we kind of want to live together and Queens is a bit of a drive from our place in Manhattan."

"So you guys want to move out together?" I supply.

"I totally don't have to, though, if you need me to stay," she rushes.

"That's alright. I was thinking of maybe moving to Hell's Kitchen anyway. I could just grab the Lincoln Tunnel and take the 495 straight to ABT. I'm more in the middle that way."

"Yeah, Jersey is a bit of a stretch from Manhattan."

"So you two are getting pretty serious then, huh?"

"I guess we are." Mel smiles.

"Is that all you wanted to talk about?"

"I guess, yeah. I was kind of worried you wouldn't want me to leave you."

"If I were staying in Manhattan, I probably wouldn't. I mean, I can't afford our place on my own, but Hell's Kitchen is much cheaper, so I should be fine. Besides, I'll be making double now that I'm dancing with both companies. Don't worry about me." I give her a smile.

"He's been asking about you."

"Yeah?"

"Just if I've been talking to you and how you're doing, that kind of stuff," Mel answers.

"Oh, I guess I could send him a postcard from Demark when I send yours," I ponder.

"Don't do that. I mean, he'd love it, but that's the problem. He needs to move on, Ames. He ended things with Harper when he got back and hasn't seen anyone since."

"Damn it, I told him not to do that," I curse.

"Bonner and I have been trying to set him up with some girls, but he won't even consider the thought."

"That's flattering and all, but I mean, I hate the idea of him holding out for something that may never happen. I love my life right now—the freedom to do whatever I want. I'm not tied down."

"I know," Mel replies quietly.

"Well, I need to get to bed. It's after midnight here and we leave for the airport in six hours." I glance at my watch.

"I miss you, Ames, but I'm glad you're happy."

"And I'm glad you're happy." I blow her a kiss.

We take a plane to Denmark rather than driving back through Germany. We spend an afternoon at the Tivoli Gardens amusement park, and then another at Legoland. This week's postcard is of the Little Mermaid sculpture.

The trip from Denmark to Sweden has to be by far my favourite. Believe it or not, you can actually drive across the Baltic Sea on this crazy bridge called the Oresund Bridge. That architect must have been a genius; you drive over the water for about five miles to an artificial island. Then you enter a tunnel that travels under the sea for another two and a half miles.

There is a lot of driving involved in Sweden, since it's such a long spread out country. That's okay, though, because I'm burning out and could use that time to sleep. We spend a couple of days in Stockholm, which is made up of fourteen different islands, so there are tons of bridges. Our last night is spent in the Ice Hotel, which is way up at the top of the country over two hundred kilometres north of the Arctic Circle. The entire thing is rebuilt every year from snow and ice. Naturally, that's the postcard I choose to send to Mel.

Our last stop during the last week of August is Norway. I'm a huge fan of the show *Vikings*, which is based on Scandinavian history, so I was definitely looking forward to seeing the real thing. The entire country is just one gorgeous landscape between the mountains, glaciers, and fjords. My favourite, I think, would be the Geirangerfjord, which looks like it came straight from the TV show. I also loved all the museums containing real Viking boats and artefacts.

There are so many other countries I'd love to see, but apparently that's the other half of the tour this winter. The cast usually returns back to New York for the fall season, where they do a few shows, and then they hit the road again until the spring season.

When we return to the states, we get a week off before the beginning of fall training. I thought about going down south to visit Mel and Bonner, but I figure I'm better off giving Dawson space. Instead, I spend the week sleeping off the jetlag and sheer exhaustion of dancing so many shows.

Mel and Bonner arrive on the first of September. I help them move into their new place in Queens, and then Mel goes apartment-hunting with me in Hell's Kitchen. I need to be moved before rehearsals pick up for both shows because I won't have time to even breathe after that.

I end up settling on a two-bedroom place in the Clinton Apartment Complex. It's much smaller than our other apartment, but I doubt I'll be spending much time there, anyway.

By the second week of September, classes are in full swing at both companies. I spend Mondays, Wednesdays, and Fridays at ABT, and Tuesdays, Thursdays, and Saturdays at NYCB. Sunday's are spent wherever I feel I need the most practice.

The cast list is posted at NYCB for *The Nutcracker*, and once again I'm the Sugar Plum Fairy. I already know the part, thankfully, so that makes doing two shows easier, since I don't have to learn two sets of choreography.

I'm surprised to see my name listed beside the part of Juliet at ABT. I'm only new, so I wasn't expecting to get the lead. My Romeo is a guy named Leonard, who's gay, which is awesome. I won't have to deal with another Damian.

"We bought tickets today for *Romeo and Juliet*." Mel plops down on my couch one Saturday night in late November.

"I could have gotten you comp ones," I protest.

"I didn't mean for us," Mel laughs.

"My mother and Dawson are coming up for Christmas, and they want to see you in action," Bonner clarifies.

"But they're coming to *The Nutcracker*, aren't they?" I scoot my legs up underneath me. My feet have been freezing lately.

"Yeah, they want to go to both," Mel answers.

"Dawson's coming too?" I get butterflies thinking about seeing him again.

"He says he won't try anything. He just wants to see you dance," Bonner assures.

"Stress me out a little more, why don't you?" I take a big gulp of wine from my glass.

"Looks like you're already stressing out more than you should be," Mel mumbles.

"What's that supposed to mean?" I turn to her.

"Just that I'm becoming worried about you—you're really skinny."

"So are you," I counter.

"You've lost a good fifteen pounds since the spring season."

"Because I had a crazy summer. I'm just in better shape now."

"How much do you weigh?"

"One fifteen," I answer, staring into my glass.

"Bullshit. How much?" Mel spits while Bonner remains quiet.

"Fine—the last time I weighed myself, I think I was like ninety-six or something." I shrug like it's nothing.

"Holy crap, Ames. You know how unhealthy that is and how dangerous—"

"I'm fine, I'll just eat more."

"I think you need to leave one of the companies. Two is too much."

"No, I have it all worked out."

"Do I need to tell Miss Taylor?" Mel asks, referring to the head nurse at NYCB. She'd pull me from the show if she knew how much I weighed.

"Jesus, Mel, it's not like I'm doing it on purpose. I don't have an eating disorder or anything. I just work so much I don't have a lot of time to eat. Then I end up burning more calories than I consume. I'll just eat more," I insist.

"I'm giving you until after the show. If you haven't gained any weight by then, I'm going to Miss Taylor."

"Fine, go right ahead. I'll be leaving on tour with ABT by then anyway." I stand up and walk to my kitchen. Laying my still-full wine glass on the counter, I walk past Mel and Bonner and straight into my room, closing the door behind me.

Chapter Twelve

AMELIA

I do try to make a point of eating more, especially high-calorie foods, but unfortunately it doesn't seem to be making much of a difference. Mel has barely spoken to me since I walked out of the room that night a couple weeks ago. I see her around NYCB and we have rehearsals together occasionally, but she doesn't encourage conversation.

It's the week leading up to the shows; luckily *The Nutcracker* is on the weekends while *Romeo and Juliet* is during the week, so they don't overlap. We are doing a run-through for staging the night before the opening, and Damian has me lifted up in the air for our final lift. I come down heavier than I was anticipating, landing on my pointe the wrong way. My foot gives out, landing me on the floor.

"Oh my god, Ame!" Mel rushes over. She had been standing at the side with the other Spanish dancers.

"I'm fine." I brush her and Damian off as they try to help me up.

"Are you sure?" Damian looks like he wants to throw up. He thinks he's responsible for injuring the Sugar Plum Fairy. My understudy isn't nearly as good as I am, which he would have to adjust to if she were to dance instead of me.

"Yeah, I just landed funny." I walk around the stage stretching out my ankle.

"That's the end of your part, anyway—go see the nurse," Leona the head director tells me.

"Do you want me to come with you?" Mel asks.

"Why, so you can tell her how much I weigh?" I snap. Trying not to limp, I walk offstage and head to the nurse's station.

Miss Taylor informs me it's probably an aggravated stress fracture in my foot. She strongly advises me to stay off it, but ultimately doesn't pull me from the show.

The following night, I'm in my dressing room after curtain call when there's a knock on the door. I open it to find Bonner holding a bouquet of roses.

"Mel's down the hall," I say, pointing.

"I know. I was already in to see her. These are from Dawson—he wasn't sure if you'd want to see him or not." Bonner holds out the bouquet.

"Thanks, I didn't even spot him in the audience." I go about removing my make-up.

"Yeah, you seemed pretty distracted. You didn't dance like you normally do."

"Why do you say that?" I ask cautiously.

"Well, I didn't notice it, but Dawson did. He hasn't stopped asking if you're alright. He insists there's something wrong."

"You can tell him I'm fine." I cross the room to change out of my tutu and leotard.

"Then why are you limping, and why is your foot taped up?"

"It's nothing, just a stress fracture." I'm growing impatient.

"Melanie is really worried about you, Amelia. We all are."

"I'd say about seventy-five percent of the dancers out there tonight had some form of minor injury. It comes with the territory. Our bodies have taken a beating these last few months. I'm working doubly as hard as them, so I'm bound to show some wear and tear. Nobody else noticed a difference in my dancing. I don't know why Dawson would."

"I don't want to fight with you about this, but Melanie asked me to make sure you're alright."

"Thanks for the concern, but I'm fine. I have to go, I need to get more studio time in before *Romeo and Juliet* tomorrow night." I shoulder past him and take the back exit.

The following night, I play the part of Juliet. It's opening night and there's a buzz in the air. All the other dancers are high on the energy, but I couldn't be bothered. To be honest, I kind of just want to go home and go to bed. I'm exhausted and my foot is bothering me.

I keep a smile plastered on my face all night, but as soon as I enter my dressing room, it disappears. Dawson is standing there, staring at me. Gone are the cast and neck brace, but he does have a cane, which he's leaning on.

"What are you doing here?" I stutter.

"Are you okay? And don't give me some bullshit answer, because I know you. What's going on, Amelia?" He holds nothing back.

"Nothing, I'm just tired," I shrug.

"I can see it in your dancing. It's more than just exhaustion."

"I have a small stress fracture in my foot. It's nothing I haven't had before."

"It's bothering you, though. I could tell by how you carried yourself."

"Why do you think you know me better than anyone else? Huh? Bonner said the same thing yesterday, that you could 'tell something was wrong,'" I air quote. "You don't know me, Dawson. It's been a year and so much has changed. I am not the same person."

"You're right, you aren't the same person. The Amelia I knew would have listened to her friends when they told her to take it easy. You're pushing yourself too hard and it's showing. You warned me not to ride because I may seriously hurt myself. This is me returning the favour."

"Fuck you," I spit.

"I'm serious, Amelia. If you aren't careful, you could do irreparable damage to your foot and you may never dance again. You can only push your body so far before it snaps."

"Because you're a fine one to talk—you can't even walk anymore."

"Exactly! I'm speaking from experience here. I didn't listen to you, and look what happened. I'm trying to prevent this from happening to you." He motions to his cane.

"Goodbye, Dawson." I walk into the bathroom in my dressing room and close the door. I lean against the wall then slide down it so that I'm sitting on the floor. I pull my knees to my chest and cry.

When I exit sometime later, Dawson is gone, and I find myself disappointed.

I grow wearier with every recital. By closing night, I'm drained. I return to my apartment and sleep for a solid twenty-four hours. Mel won't answer my texts and I don't want to go over there because Anna May and Dawson are staying at her place for the holidays.

I end up spending Christmas alone, which gives me time to think. I'm not enjoying ballet anymore; it feels more like a chore, which makes me sad. I decide dancing with both companies is too much, so before I leave on tour with ABT, I drop my resignation off at NYCB.

As I'm boarding the plane, I get a text from Mel.

> MELANIE: You weren't even going to tell me you were quitting?

> AMELIA: You didn't seem all that concerned with my decisions anymore.

I send my reply before turning off my phone for takeoff.

Ireland is our first stop. We are still performing *Romeo and Juliet*, which I've grown tired of. I try to enjoy the local pubs and all the greenery, but my thoughts keep drifting elsewhere.

The same thing happens in the United Kingdom. I can't bring myself to have fun like before. We fly to Italy, where the others indulge in Italian cuisine. By the time we reach Austria, I'm sick of everyone and everything. I'm pretty sure the others can tell, because nobody really speaks to me anymore. Hungary, Romania, and Ukraine pass in a blur; I spend most of the time offstage asleep on the tour bus, not bothering to participate in anything with the cast. Belarus is the final destination, and I'm beyond ready to go home.

I head straight to Mel and Bonner's place when I get back, not even bothering to go home first. It's not until I get there that I remember it's spring break, so they're probably down south.

I run home long enough to repack and book a plane ticket. I hail the first cab I see and then I hop on a plane to Texas.

DAWSON

Strider trots beneath me as I help my dad round up the cows to move them to their spring pasture. My father and I have never had a very open relationship. He's a quiet man who likes to keep to himself. He's an extremely hard worker, which means he takes on more at the ranch than he probably should for his age. Unfortunately, that means he's kind of tied to the place. If he were to leave for even a day, the place would fall apart. He never came to see me in the hospital after my accident, which sucked, but I understood why.

It's times like this one, though, that I appreciate his silence. Since I came back from New York after Christmas, I haven't been up for a whole lot of talking. I jump at every opportunity to work with my father because it means a day of quiet—especially now that my brother and Melanie are back for spring break; they try too hard to set me up with women. I'm not interested, but they won't take no for an answer.

The sun is setting when we finally return to the barn. Dad goes straight to the house, but I take the time to rub down the horses and settle them in for the night. I hear someone walking across the driveway and into the barn.

"I'm not in the mood, Bonner." I sigh without turning around.

"I guess I'll come back, then." A voice I've been dreaming of for months speaks up behind me.

I turn around and Amelia is standing in the doorway, staring down at the dirt.

"I didn't know you were here," I finally say after an awkward silence.

"I got back from Europe this morning. I flew straight here."

"Why?"

"Because you were right," she admits.

"About what?"

"There was something wrong that night of the show. I just didn't know it yet."

"They took you out of the show for your foot, didn't they?" Of course the only reason she'd come here is because she couldn't dance anymore.

"No, my foot is fine. I'm still with ABT for now."

"For now?" I question.

"Ballet doesn't make me happy anymore. The night you spoke to me after *Romeo and Juliet*, I realized that. I quit NYCB in hopes that maybe I was just tired from working with both companies, that the European tour would make me feel better. But if anything, I think it made my decision all the clearer."

"What are you saying?"

"I've never been as happy as when I'm here, when I'm with you. When I walked away from you over a year ago, I thought it was because I needed to grow as an individual. I thought my happiness was dependant on you, but that's not it at all. I am capable of being happy without you. I just prefer having you there to share it with me. You are my home, my safe place, where I feel most as peace with myself. I love you, Dawson, and this is where I belong. I still love to dance, but not as much as I love you."

Dropping the reins that I was still holding, I limp across the stable to Amelia, pull her towards me, and kiss her.

"I love you too, but are you sure? Dance is your passion."

"It still can be—working my ass off for perfection takes that away, though. It no longer gives me the freedom it used to."

"So you're staying?" I ask as she blinks those long lashes up at me with those emerald eyes that I missed so much.

"I am. This is where I belong." She hugs me again, so I squeeze her tightly to my chest. Everything feels right again for the first time in almost two years.

CPSIA information can be obtained
at www.ICGtesting.com
Printed in the USA
LVHW090245091019
633650LV00003B/753/P

9 781525 555787